THE COCAINE PRINCESS 10

King Rio

Lock Down Publications and Ca$h
Presents
The Cocaine Princess 10
A Novel by *King Rio*

Lock Down Publications

P.O. Box 944
Stockbridge, Ga 30281
www.lockdownpublications.com

Copyright 2023 by King Rio
The Cocaine Princess 10

Lock Down Publications
Like our page on Facebook: Lock Down Publications @
www.facebook.com/lockdownpublications.ldp
Book interior design by: **Shawn Walker**

Stay Connected with Us!

Text **LOCKDOWN** to 22828 to stay up-to-date with new releases, sneak peaks, contests and more…

Thank you!

Submission Guideline.

Submit the first three chapters of your completed manuscript to ldpsubmissions@gmail.com, subject line: Your book's title. The manuscript must be in a .doc file and sent as an attachment. Document should be in Times New Roman, double spaced and in size 12 font. Also, provide your synopsis and full contact information. If sending multiple submissions, they must each be in a separate email.

Have a story but no way to send it electronically? You can still submit to LDP/Ca$h Presents. Send in the first three chapters, written or typed, of your completed manuscript to:

LDP: Submissions Dept
P.O. Box 944
Stockbridge, Ga 30281

DO NOT send original manuscript. Must be a duplicate.

Provide your synopsis and a cover letter containing your full contact information.

Thanks for considering LDP and Ca$h Presents.

Dedication:

In loving memory of Angela Rabotte

Acknowledgements

First and foremost I must thank God for blessing me with the time and talent to write these books. I'm forever grateful.

To my family and friends who push me to keep going even when I say I'm done, I'll never quit writing just because I love to make you all proud.

Next up, my readers. I know I don't know all of you but here's a list of the ones I do know. Thank you all so much for the support. I won't quit! :)

Linda Taft, Nikolai Konstantin, Jenell Proctor, Taquila Thompson, Pam and Quateisha Williams, Donica James, Dawn Avery, Cody West, Christine Denise, Shae Weaver, Lynetta Denson-Hart, Karlton and Tori Benson, Latasha Mack, Tarina Wright, Twanica Bonneau Hazel, Consuela "Tangie" Bryant, Antoinette Mitchell-Tate, Shay Wright, Shannon Barnett, Farshawna Crook, Amy Annette Gillespie Withers, Ashley Hicks, Nik Nicole, Debbi Kowalik, Sharlene Smith (my wonderful promoter), Cree Owens, Rosezenia Cummings, Tamara Hope, Quita Boger, Schawanna Morris, Stephanie Denise, Doris Buchanan-Beans, Melonie Frazier, and Shay Cooper.
If I forgot your name feel free to add it here _____.
To my fellow authors, I wish you all a ton of success. Write every day no matter what and success will be sure to find you.
May God bless us all.

Prologue

Lakita "Bubbles" Thomas was naked and trembling in fear.

Being hung upside down by her ankles from the ceiling of an abandoned warehouse in lower Manhattan wasn't how she'd expected her day to go when she woke up this morning.

There was a strip of duct tape on her mouth. The heavy chain tied around her ankles hurt like hell. Her head was maybe five feet from the ground, and she was swinging from side to side, propelled by gentle pushes from Alexus every time she reached her and Enrique every time she reached him.

Fifty heavily armed men in black suits stood along the walls, and Bubbles saw dozens more standing outside around the red fleet of SUVs they'd arrived to her home in. She'd been taking her morning bath when they came crashing through her front door, Alexus leading the way, Enrique seconds behind the ruthless young billionaire cartel boss, barking orders at their men.

Luckily, Bubbles had managed to leave her daughter with her mother in Chicago just eight hours before Alexus found her. She was sobbing miserably, but the fact that her daughter was safe calmed her a little...just enough to start looking around for a way out of the troubling situation she'd somehow managed to get herself into.

Chapter 1

Alexus Costilla had taken possession of Lakita "Bubbles" Thomas's smartphone as soon as she'd seen it resting on a charging pad in the thick girl's living room.

Bubbles was Alexus's husband's side chick — one of them, at least — and since he'd changed his phone numbers and disappeared on her a few days ago, she hadn't heard from him since. Kidnapping Bubbles was the logical thing to do. Blake loved Bubbles. There was no doubt in Alexus's mind that she would find his new phone numbers in the big-bootied ex-stripper's phone.

And sure enough, here it was. Saved under "Blakey". Same area code as his prior phones.

"This black mother..." Alexus said as she dialed his number and gave Bubbles another rough push.

He answered: "What up, big booty?"

"You sneaky little fucker," Alexus muttered heatedly. She shoved harder when the swinging girl made it back to her. "Do you honestly think you can just leave me like that? Did you think I wouldn't find your little slut?"

"Baby...calm down," Blake said.

"No, you bring your ass home. That's all there is to it. Either you come home or Ms. Bubbles is history. I want you in New York by noon. I'll meet you at JFK."

Alexus ended the call before Blake could say another word. She turned the phone off and put it in her red leather Chanel shoulder bag, which also held the heavy, goldplated .50-caliber Desert Eagle handgun she was known to carry. The bag matched her cherry-red, skintight Chanel dress and Louboutin heels.

She'd only recently started wearing red as a sign of vengeance against her husband's many mistresses.

Her heels click-clacked across the cold concrete as she went to a chair that stood against the north wall. She dragged it back to the upside down woman and sat down. Her frigid green eyes were like a pendulum, swinging with the woman's face.

"I hope I don't have to kill you today," Alexus said, glancing at her red diamond Rolex watch for the time.

It was 9:35 AM Eastern time.

"If Blake's not at that airport in two hours and twenty-five minutes," she said, "I may have to do just that."

Chapter 2

Mercedes Costilla was getting tired of being mistaken for her sister Alexus.

She was jogging down Michigan Avenue with her younger sister Porsche Clark. The driver of the black Mercedes Sprinter van they'd arrived in was parked ten blocks down at the Gucci store, which is where their mile-long run would come to an end.

The two black Escalades cruising alongside them were full of 4 Corner Hustlers, the gang that Mercedes and Porsche grew up around on Chicago's west side. The youngsters — five teenaged boys and three girls who weren't much older — toted guns that were as big as they were. They were a growing squad of gang members whose main priority was protecting Mercedes.

She enjoyed having them around her all day. It was like a season of Making The Band — all Mercedes did was give orders, provide food and shelter, and monitor their schedules to make certain that they were properly distributing the drugs she routinely gave them to keep their neighborhood flooded with cocaine, heroin, and weed.

On mornings like this when Chicago police were busy kicking in doors and responding to the endless shootings that plagued the Windy City, Mercedes always went out for a run with her security nearby for protection, usually in a section of the city that rarely suffered from the chaos of gang wars.

The Magnificent Mile was the perfect spot for a peaceful run.

Struggling to keep up, Porsche said, "Bitch, if you don't slow the fuck down. I'm damn near 'bout to have a heart attack."

"That's from all that smoking and drinking you and Sasha do all day," Mercedes reasoned. "Maybe if you cut back on that bullshit you might get in shape like me."

"Don't nobody wanna be like you." Porsche rolled her eyes and stopped to catch her breath. She was a slender-bodied girl, unlike Mercedes, who had all the hips and ass in the world.

Porsche wasn't being a hundred percent honest. Everyone wanted to be like Mercedes. She was a young, bad 22-year-old with a net worth of $47 million. She and her billionaire sister were all the tabloids talked about.

Mercedes turned to face Porsche, jogging in place. "Come on, slowpoke."

"Wait a minute, bitch."

"I ain't got a minute. We gotta get that work to Bear and Tremaine by noon, and before that we gotta take showers and go shopping for Nell's baby shower. Now, come on."

Mercedes looked at her Apple watch before they took off running again. She'd burned enough calories for the day. She was trying to lose the few extra pounds she'd gained over the past month. There was a slight pudge in her belly that had to go.

When they started off again they didn't stop until they were at the luxury Mercedes van.

During the run Mercedes ruminated over the money she was chasing today. Bear, another 4CH from her old neighborhood, had $18,000 for a half kilo of coke. Tremaine, a Blackstone gang member from the south side, had $30,000 for a half kilo of heroin. There were also several of her guys who needed more drugs, and a dirty cop who wanted in on the millions he knew she was making on the west side.

She'd gotten word that Tremaine was a federal informant, so she wasn't sure how she'd deal with him. Sometimes federal informants only wired up when they were on the hook for some crime, but Mercedes wasn't into taking chances. She knew that she would have to be as cold-hearted as the rest of Chicago's infamous gang bosses.

There was a shower in the luxury van. Mercedes was the first to get in. She was quick, choosing to merely soap up and rinse rather than taking her time like she usually did. Kita, her hairstylist, was waiting on her when she got out of the shower. She sat down and got her hair whipped up while Porsche showered.

Kita was as skinny as Porsche. She was a south side girl who'd moved out west in her senior year of high school after her father was shot and killed in Englewood. As she was curling Mercedes's hair she asked about Alexus.

"Don't mention that bitch to me. Please," Mercedes said. She hated her sister with a passion.

"Well, excuse me. I mean, she is your sister and all. I just wanted to know what was up with Bulletface. His fine ass."

"Blake's tired of her ass, too. That's why he keeps cheating on her every time she turns her back. The bitch is a lunatic, Kita. I mean seriously. She had my momma killed because my mom's name was Whitney and Blake cheated on her with a girl named Whitney."

"He slept with your momma?"

"No, stupid," Mercedes said. "The girl he cheated with was another Whitney. Remember the Whitney murders?"

Kita shook her head no.

"Well," Mercedes said, "when Alexus sent her guys at the girl Blake had cheated with, she didn't know exactly which Whitney he had fucked, so Alexus had every Whitney in his city killed. My momma happened to be one of them."

"Wow. That's cold."

"Tell me about it." Mercedes shook her head. "Then Blake got into it with my baby daddy and had him killed."

"I remember that. Duke was his name, right?"

"Yeah. Blake had knocked him out one day when me and Duke was fighting. Duke got back at him backstage at a concert one day and Blake had him killed for it. It happened the same night Blake's dumb ass accidentally killed my daddy."

"Girl, you done had it rough."

"Yeah, but I'm good now. Fuck it. At least I'm rich." Mercedes shrugged. "Only thing I hate is the whole drug cartel thing. I'm sure you've seen it on the news. Alexus is crazy as fuck and I don't want anything to do with her or the rest of my daddy's family. I didn't even know I was related to them until I was eighteen, and ever sense then it's like I've been cursed."

"I remember when you lost your kids," Kita said.

The memory of her children's deaths brought tears to Mercedes's soft green eyes. No matter how many days and months passed by, she could never forget the sheer joy her children had brought her during their brief time on earth. Baby Duke and

Meyoncé had been murdered by Jennifer Costilla, Mercedes and Alexus's aunt, the woman who'd been named public enemy number one by the United States government all the way up until the night she was killed by Alexus's men at Blake's Highland Park mansion.

Mercedes squeezed her eyes shut to erase the tears. The memory of her murdered children would forever be a source of heartache, but she was getting better at holding it in.

"I'm sorry," Kita said.

"It's fine. Sometimes I need to vent, you know. It's always bottled up inside me."

"I understand exactly what you mean. When my dad got killed I cried just about every day for a year straight. You can never get over that kind of hurt. It'll be with you every day and night. Trust me, I've been through it."

Sniffling, Mercedes shook her head and examined her hairdo in her portable mirror. As always, Kita had done her right. She dug in her purse and peeled off five crisp Benjamins from a rubber-banded bundle of cash. She handed them to Kita, who tucked the $500 in her bra and kept right on doing her thing.

Mercedes was out of the chair and getting dressed when Porsche came out of the shower. She put on a black Prada jumpsuit and black five-inch heels. The Jesus piece on her thin gold necklace had black diamonds in its face, as did her tennis bracelet and Michael Kors watch. She wore black every day in the same way that her sister Alexus wore white...though recently Alexus had been spotted out several times wearing all red, for some unknown reason.

"I wonder what has Alexus wearing red all of a sudden," Mercedes said, more to herself than anything as she went to Instagram and looked at her sister's page.

There were only two pictures of Alexus in red. She wore white in all the others. Her most recent pic was a selfie showing off her red-polished fingernails and red lipstick.

"She's beautiful like you," Kita said, looking over Mercedes's shoulder at the photo.

"We look like twins," Mercedes said. "I hate that shit. Everywhere I go people think I'm her. It's funny because we only have the same daddy. Apparently his genes were the strongest."

"Y'all do look just alike." Kita opened up a window before dousing Mercedes's do with hairspray. "It's not a bad thing, though. She's a bad bitch. Gotta admit that. She's killing the game. Nobody ever thought we'd have a bigger celebrity than Queen Bey until Queen A came along. How much is she worth now?"

Mercedes shrugged. "$70 billion, I think. Maybe a little more. I don't know. I don't keep track."

"She has her own damn TV networks. You should get us a show, girl. For real. I'd entertain the hell out of people."

"I've been thinking about it. Maybe I can do something like Real Housewives of Chicago," Mercedes said thoughtfully.

Kita laughed. "Yeah, right. And do what, show how everybody gets killed around here? Forget that, we need to take our asses to Miami, or Los Angeles. Somewhere safe where we can film without getting our camera crews robbed at gunpoint."

Mercedes was laughing as she got out of what she'd grown fond of calling "the beauty chair" and let Porsche take her seat.

"About damn time," Porsche muttered snidely. "For a minute I thought my hair was gon' be all jacked up when we got to the mall."

"Oh, shut up. Hire your own stylist and maybe you wouldn't have that problem." Mercedes went to her usual seat and flipped open the laptop computer. She decided that no time was better than now to send out the email for her reality show proposal. "Kita, would you really be on the show with us if I made it happen?"

"Girl, what kind of question is that? Hell yes, I would be on the show. That's instant fame right there. Even if it's canceled I could fuck around and get my own spinoff show. I'm all in, just give me the word."

Mercedes began typing an email to Alexus's mother, knowing that she'd have a better chance with Rita than with Alexus.

The Sprinter van was soaring up Lake Shore Drive ahead of the two Escalades. It was a warm summer day in late April, which meant fun in the sun for most cities but killing season here in "Chiraq". Mercedes had started to like cruising this scenic route once she'd become a millionaire. People always knew it was her in the white Maybach Landaulet, which was now painted black like the one she'd bought Porsche.

She happened to look out her window at the towering skyscrapers just as her iPhone rang.

She was surprised to see that it was Alexus calling.

Instinctively, she ignored the call, frowning at the phone.

Just then, Porsche said, "I'm telling you, Cedes, I got a feeling this summer is going to get a lot worse. These young Chicago niggas ain't for none. I bet at least seven or eight bodies get dropped this weekend alone."

Little did either of them know, there would be a lot more than seven or eight bodies dropped this weekend, and some of them would be members of their own squad.

Chapter 3

Blake's nerves were a wreck.

He sat alone on his Gulfstream 650 private jet, smoking blunt after blunt of Kush and drinking ounce after ounce of Promethazine with Codeine and Faygo soda on ice.

He couldn't stop checking the New York news websites on his laptop computer.

"What made me marry that psycho," he muttered aloud to himself.

He'd given Nona $200,000 in cash and a first-class ticket to Los Angeles, which is where she'd wanted to go. It was enough money to start her on the path to the new identity she believed she needed to stay safe from Alexus and the Costilla Cartel.

With things going the way they were, he'd had no choice but to send her away.

There were no news updates of a gruesomely murdered woman so he believed Bubbles still had hope.

He thought back to several weeks ago when Alexus had sent a group of killers after his side piece, Tasia "Baddie Barbie" Olsen", an Atlanta stripper an old business associate named Cup had hooked him up with.

Now it was rumored that Barbie was in the FBI's witness protection program following an incident where her sister was shot and two Atlanta policemen were killed.

Blake hadn't heard from Barbie ever since.

He went to his Facebook page, which had well over fifty million followers. It was the page for Bulletface, the name under which he'd become a world-famous rap star, CEO of Money Bagz Management and a spokesperson for Reebok, though he rarely ever wore their products outside of photo shoots and planned outings where the media was certain to find him for photo opportunities.

He dumped out the remaining $250,000 in packets of hundreds from his Louis Vuitton duffle bag on the table in front of him before utilizing his selfie stick for a pic of himself with the pile of cash before him.

With the picture he posted:

'More money, more problems. #TheKing'

Tens of thousands of Facebook likes and comments ensued.

He didn't waste his time reading them. Instead he eased back in the white leather seat and plotted on a way to save his side chick from his ruthless wife.

Alexus was indeed a ruthless woman.

Just a week and a half ago she'd blown out the brains of his son Junior's mother's closest friend. She'd done it right in front of him, as if the grisly murder were a regular part of their daily routine.

The image of Danielle's brainless skull was still vivid in his mind.

"She gotta honor a divorce after all this crazy shit," he said, again to himself. He wanted nothing more to do with his wife. She was half Black and half Mexican. The Black half Blake could deal with. It was her Mexican side that troubled him. She was the boss of Mexico's most violent and wealthy drug cartel. Being married to Alexus Costilla was like being married to Griselda Blanco. Before he'd accidentally killed her father, Juan "Papi" Costilla, Blake had gone through hell dealing with the old man. One day Papi had barged into Blake's Miami home with his armed soldiers and carrying a blood-soaked backpack with a severed head in it. Blake had held Papi at gunpoint with an AK-47, while Papi's men aimed guns at Blake's squad. It had been the head of a young black boy, a family member of an MTN News anchorman named Nat Turner who dated Rita at the time.

Now, Alexus was beginning to show all the telltale signs of Papi.

Brutal killings ordered on the regular.

Homicidal tendencies.

Yeah, Alexus had definitely taken after her father.

Staring out the oval window to the left of his seat, Blake wondered what he was going to do when he landed at JFK. He had an AR-15 and a 9-millimeter Glock with a 50-round drum magazine in it. The guns were in a hidden compartment in his snow-white Rolls-Royce Phantom, which was soaring through the clouds somewhere behind the Gulfstream on his Boeing 747.

He contemplated the possibility of having to use the guns on Alexus and her men all the way up to the minute his plane landed at JFK at exactly 11:49 AM Eastern standard time.

Chapter 4

Alexus had a chainsaw in her hands, revving it up and getting ready to disembowel Bubbles, when Enrique's phone rang at 11:54.

"He's here," Enrique said after answering his smartphone. He told the guy on the line to bring Blake to the warehouse and then ended the call.

Handing Enrique the chainsaw, Alexus gave Bubbles a sharp smack to the face. "It's your lucky day, Little Miss Bubbles. It truly is." She waved for her men to get the girl down and told them to chain her to the chair.

"I thought it was about to get all messy," Enrique said. He turned off the chainsaw and put it on the floor with his steel prosthetic hand.

Alexus crossed her arms over her chest and glowered at Bubbles as she was put in the chair by two brawny Mexican men. There was something about Bubbles that made Alexus not want to kill her, but Alexus couldn't quite put her finger on what it was.

Maybe it was because Bubbles was a big-buttocked redbone with a pretty face, just like Alexus was. Or it could be the fact that Alexus knew that Bubbles was the mother of one child like she was. Whatever the case, Alexus wasn't feeling as cold-hearted as she'd thought she would feel when she finally crossed paths again with Bubbles.

"Take the tape off her mouth," Alexus said. "I wanna get an understanding with this bitch before she makes me go at her sideways."

Enrique walked over and ripped the tape off the girl's mouth.

"If you start crying and shit I'll kill you for being a coward," Alexus threatened.

Bubbles struggled to keep a straight face. "I wasn't even with him."

"I know that. Where's the Nona bitch?"

"They didn't tell—"

"Lie and I'll kill you for that, too."

Bubbles paused, rethinking her statement. Apparently she wanted to live. She glanced around at all the armed men.

"Go on," Alexus persisted.

"Last I heard they were in Hawaii together. Think he has a new beach house out there. But I promise that's all I know. Look, please don't hurt me. I'm all my daughter has. I already told Blake that we're done. I'm—"

"That's enough," Alexus said, cutting Bubbles off and going back to staring at her iPhone 6 Plus.

She had just tried phoning Mercedes a few minutes ago in regards to a memory that had just surfaced in her brain. It was something Mercedes had told her about Baddie Barbie — another of Blake's side chicks — just before the Indianapolis hotel bombing that had hospitalized the both of them.

She dialed Mercedes's number twice more and got no answer.

"I know this bitch sees me calling," Alexus murmured as she composed a text message to Mercedes.

'Don't nobody wanna talk to yo funky, funny actin ass bitch I'm tryna ask u an important question answer the fuckin phone'

A smirk crossed her face as she hit send.

Seconds later she got a call back.

"Bitch, who is you callin' funny actin'?!" Mercedes said. "Just because I don't wanna talk to you—"

"Whatever, you called my lawyer asking me to save your so-called friends," Alexus cut in. "If I wanna call you I can do it whenever the fuck I please."

"Bitch, what do you want?"

Alexus's smirk broadened. "Remember on the elevator before the hotel blast? You told me something about that bitch Blake's been fucking. The Barbie bitch. What's up with her?"

Mercedes paused for a long moment.

"Well?" Alexus pressed.

"I was just talking about this with Porsche. Barbie and her sister Fanny were plotting on Blake. They're your old friend Tasia's sisters. Well, Jantasia. Tasia is actually Barbie, the youngest sister. Jantasia is the one who went missing with Cereniti in Mexico, but when you knew her we all called her Tasia, not knowing that her name was actually Jantasia."

"So," Alexus asked, studying her captive's tear-streaked face, "Barbie was plotting on Blake the whole time? Wow. And his dumb ass was making love to the bitch."

Alexus couldn't believe it. Her anger at Blake's side chicks was turning out to be a good thing after all.

"I heard Cup's mad at Blake about something," she said, her unwavering stare fixed on Bubbles. "You heard anything?"

Mercedes hesitated. "He, um...he thinks Blake had his clubs shot up. At least that's what I think. I don't know. Look, I want a reality show on MTN. Think you can make that happen for me? Big sister?"

"Lay it on thick." Alexus rolled her eyes. "If that's what you want, sure. No problem. Call my mom. I'll approve it. As long as it meets our requirements and doesn't look downright ridiculous, I'm all in. You'd better start calling me, though. I am your sister."

"I'll start calling."

"You better." Mending the damaged relationship she and her sister had put a smile on Alexus's face. "I'll call you back. Let me deal with Blake's cheating ass first."

When Alexus ended the call she was suddenly certain that she'd let Bubbles live. If only for the sake of the daughter.

But she would have some fun first.

She rolled a blunt of Kush and paced from one end of the warehouse to the other, smoking it and thinking about a dozen cartel related things while she waited on Blake to show up.

She currently had two submarines on the way to the California coast, each hauling 12,000 kilos of cocaine. The bricks of coke would be delivered to the many Black and Mexican gangs in America that depended on the Costilla Cartel for their narcotics. Alexus hardly ever did anything more than give a few orders a day to keep her cartel up and running. For the most part, the criminal organization ran itself. Especially with Enrique giving all the war orders and numerous accountants calculating and managing expenses.

There was so much cash coming in that Alexus was having a hard time stashing it all. She had billions of dollars in cash stuffed inside a hilltop mansion in Malibu, California. She had billions more hidden away in offshore accounts, and her legitimate net worth was over $70 billion, though most of the fortune had been accumulated illegally. The government knew it. They'd worked with her at first, but now that she was choosing to do her own thing they were turning on her.

On top of it all, she had to deal with a cheating husband who had an unlimited supply of groupies that were all willing to jump his bones in hopes of an eventual payout.

He came walking in through the warehouse's rear loading dock just minutes later, and for a moment all Alexus could do was regard him with an ice-cold glare.

She wanted so badly to reach in her bag and lift out her big golden pistol.

Blake had his duffle bag in one hand and a double-stacked Styrofoam in the other. Alexus knew it was full of Lean. It was all he'd been drinking for the past few years.

Five white diamond necklaces gleamed brilliantly on his neck. An equal number of white diamond bracelets shined on his left wrist, and the Hublot watch on his right wrist blinged just as brightly. His hair was cut low and crisply lined. His thick lips were parted just enough to show the glistening diamonds in his gold teeth. He looked so remarkably handsome that Alexus understood why so many women were after him. He was a gangster and a sex symbol, like 50 Cent had been when he first made it big. Bulletface was the most talked about rapper in history, the first billionaire in all of Hip Hop, and he never missed the chance to put it on display with his flashy jewelry and foreign cars.

"You think you're Floyd Mayweather or something," Alexus said, the right side of her upper lip raised in disgust, "and it's not cute at all."

"Let her go, Alexus," Blake said as he paused ten feet away from her and flicked his eyes around at all her men. "Stop being a psycho for just one day. Please. Damn."

Alexus's eyelids became stringent slits. She slowly walked across the floor to him. "Sounds to me like you're afraid. Is that it? Is big bad Blake getting scared of his very own wife?"

"Fuck you and these Mexican muhfuckas you got in here with you," he snapped. "The fuck I'm supposed to be scared of? I ain't never been scared of nothin', and I ain't about to start bein' scared today. Let that girl go. She ain't did shit to you and I ain't even been back with her."

"Where's the other bitch?" Alexus asked.

Blake turned to Enrique, who was holding a submachine gun with an attached sound suppressor.

"Why are you letting her do crazy shit like this?" he asked Enrique.

Enrique remained stone-faced, his expression completely indecipherable.

"Answer the question," Alexus said, planting her hands on her hips. "Where is that bitch Nona. Either you tell me where she is or this bitch will die in her place."

"Let me talk to you without all these people listening," Blake said.

Reluctantly, Alexus allowed him to lead her to a section of the warehouse where none of her men were present, but Enrique made sure to stay ten steps behind her.

She realized as she sauntered that she'd unconsciously left her Chanel bag unzipped beneath her arm.

The goldplated handle of her Desert Eagle protruded three inches out of the shoulder bag.

Blake noticed it as soon as they were standing face to face, which is when she saw the big drum on the Glock in his open duffle.

He frowned at the butt of her gun. "Why is your bag open? You wanna shoot me?"

"I should be asking you the same thing."

27

"I don't trust these Mexicans. I'm a street nigga. You can have these dudes on shoot-to-kill mode in a heartbeat. I'm blowin' next time a nigga up strap on me. I don't give a fuck who it is."

"You're so handsome." A sheen of tears were suddenly on her lower eyelids. She winked them away. "You're my husband. We're supposed to be happy, damn it! I'm not cheating on you! Why do you keep doing it to me? Am I not good enough for you?"

"Let me hug you." Blake's voice was as calm as can be.

He reached out for a hug, and for some reason Alexus fell into his arms and started bawling.

She had unexpectedly broken down.

Blake held her in a warm lover's embrace. "I love you, Alexus. I'll stay with you. Just stop killing people. We both gotta stop this shit. I'll leave the streets alone, you leave this cartel shit alone — I mean ALL the way alone — and we can live like Jay and Bey." He cradled her face in his hands and pressed his lips to her forehead, then pushed her head back to look in her eyes. "As a matter of fact, we'll live better than any couple ever. Look at all the bread we got. Together we're already number one. Let's leave all this shit alone and focus on us until our last days."

"You promise?" He had Alexus wrapped around his finger.

"I promise," he said. "I'll move back in with you and stay there forever. But you gotta give up this cartel business. We need to go all the way legit while we still got the chance. You know the feds on us. We already got billions to play with. This the best time to get out the game."

Alexus used the backs of her thumbs to wipe away her tears. Her abandoning the cartel would leave it to Mercedes, and if she turned it down the crown would be passed on to Pedro.

Mercedes was a Chicago native who'd only stepped foot in Mexico a couple of times. There was no way she'd have the support of all the Mexican soldiers.

Which is where Pedro had an advantage. He knew people all over Mexico. He was born and raised in Matamoros, and had attended college in Mexico City before dropping out and successfully trying his hand at real estate. Now he owned hundreds of multimillion dollar properties in numerous countries, and he managed it all while simultaneously dealing with the South American cartels to ensure that the Costilla Cartel kept thousands of kilos on hand for immediate distribution.

"I'll try to just leave it all to Pedro," Alexus said. "If we have to I'll scare Mercedes out of the way. She doesn't deserve to be in charge. She's a snake."

"Aw, now she's a snake? She wasn't one when you pulled that gun on me in Indianapolis? Oh, and I found out why I'm beefin' wit' Cup and them niggas in Chicago. Guess who was behind that?"

Alexus sighed. "Mercedes," she guessed.

"She sent some niggas to shoot up his clubs and had em shout "MBM Gang" before they did it."

Alexus shook her head. She zipped her bag shut. "I made a mistake. I should have known better than to trust her. Don't worry. She'll pay for everything she's done. Especially if she tries to take the reigns of the family business. She's not ready for Gamuza's men, and just the sight of the Sinaloa cartel will have her shaking in her heels."

Chapter 5

Mercedes was excited about the reality show, so excited that she burst into Porsche's bedroom to deliver the news...only to find Porsche's face buried between the thighs of her 17-year-old friend Sasha.

"What the fuck are you doing?!" Mercedes gasped in shock.

Porsche jumped out of the bed wiping the young girl's juices from her mouth and chin.

Sasha hurriedly covered her nakedness with the blanket.

"Don't you know how to knock?" Porsche said, her head slightly lowered in embarrassment.

"You nasty bitches are gay? I fucking knew it."

"We're not gay," Sasha corrected as she grabbed her panties from off a pillow and pulled them under the covers with her.

"Two women having sex is gay, isn't it?" Mercedes looked from Porsche to Sasha and back to Porsche again. "I cannot believe you, lil sis. This girl is underage."

Sasha sucked her teeth. "Please, I am grown. And just because we lick on each other every now and then don't make us gay, 'cause I love men just as much as the next bitch."

"You hoes are ignorant." Shaking her head, Mercedes turned to leave the room.

Which is when a grand idea struck her.

Something like this would be perfect for the reality show.

She stopped at the door and turned back to the two freaky young women. "I think we got the show. Y'all could have saved this stunt for the season premiere."

"The reality show? On MTN?" Porsche was immediately geeked. "Now, that's what I'm talkin' about! I'm with it!"

Mercedes gave another shake of the head as she went back out to the lavishly furnished living room of Porsche and Sasha's swanky new condo with her friends Shakema and Kita. They had been watching the full season of Power, since Mercedes had somehow managed to miss every single episode of the show half the country was obsessed with watching.

There were fourteen rolled blunts of Kush, two bottles of Ciroc vodka, a bucket of ice on a messily stacked collection of napkins, and three champagne glasses on the coffee table. Kita had one blunt fired up already.

Mercedes had leapt up and ran to Porsche's bedroom right after the call from Alexus.

Now, after having just caught her sister sucking on Sasha's pussy, Mercedes wasn't so excited.

"Girl," Kita said, "was that the TV show you was talkin' 'bout on the phone? Please tell me that was Alexus."

Mercedes plopped down between her two friends and shook her head in disgust.

Kita misunderstood the head shake. "So, it wasn't Alexus?"

"No, it was her." Mercedes said. "She said I'll probably get the show. I knew she wasn't going to just turn me down. Not after all the shit she's put me through. But forget that, I just caught Porsche—"

"What do you mean 'forget that'? This is big! A TV show!" Kita got to her feet. "I'm sorry, but you absolutely have to get me a spot somewhere in the cast. Even if I'm only on there to do your hair. I will be more than happy with that."

"Sit your ass down." Mercedes had to laugh as she snatched Kita back down to her seat.

She decided not to even tell them about what she'd just busted her younger sister doing.

Following the morning jog they'd all went shopping for their friend Nell's baby shower. Shanell Day was eight months pregnant with a daughter she made with a married Bears linebacker. He was being a deadbeat about the situation, claiming that the kid couldn't possibly be his, so Mercedes had gone overboard with the gifts, spending close to $215,000 on her soon-to-be goddaughter.

The bags were piled high on the the smooth, polished wood floor across the room from them. Strollers, walkers, bottles, pacifiers, clothes, gold and diamond necklaces and earrings, toys, diapers, food, milk, and everything else a baby needed.

Eight more of Mercedes's women friends were stringing up banners and hanging up balloons for Nell's surprise baby shower.

Mercedes said: "Do y'all know that the $215,000 I spent on gifts for Nell is the cost of just one of Alexus's perfume bottles? She wears Clive Christian. It literally costs $215,000."

Shakema shrugged. She was kind of chubby and only mildly attractive. Just the other day she'd aborted a baby due to a dispute with the baby's father. She wore a ton of makeup and a black Prada dress that was similar to the one Kita was wearing.

Mercedes had on a tiny pair of black denim shorts that were just short enough to reveal the undersides of her meaty rear cheeks. A bracelet that was replete with large black diamonds flickered on her wrist. Like her older sister's rap star husband, she was known to carry a duffle bag full of cash, and right now it was sitting next to the glass-top coffee table— a custom made black leather Chanel duffle bag containing $500,000 in hundred-dollar bills and a .40-caliber Glock with an attached 30-round clip and two extras.

There was also half a pound of OG Kush in the duffle.

All Mercedes and her friends did was smoke weed, day and night, through hard times and good times, rainy weather and sunshine. It helped soothe the scars left by the loss of her family.

She picked up a blunt from the table and lit it for herself.

"Alexus has close to a hundred billion dollars," Mercedes continued, "maybe more. It's amazing how much money she blows through, but she deserves it. I'm glad I wasn't raised around my daddy's family like she was. I'd probably be dead or in jail by now. Those cartels are insane."

"A quarter million dollars for a bottle of perfume is ridiculous," Kita said, shaking her head as she popped a Xanax pill and chased it with a shot of Ciroc. With a tightly strained expression, she added, "But if I had her money I'd blow through it, too. A bitch wouldn't be able to tell me nothin'."

Mercedes laughed again but only because she understood Alexus's perspective. Being at the very top of the world's totem pole as far as wealth, Alexus had the right to splurge on herself when she wanted to. It's what Mercedes would do if she ever managed to accumulate such a massive net worth.

But, of course, that was impossible.

Mercedes knew she'd always be beneath her long-lost big sister when it came to wealth. There was no way she could make the kind of money Alexus made as the top boss of Mexico's number-one drug cartel.

Just then, Mercedes felt her iPhone 6 vibrating in her bag.

She pulled it out and saw that again it was Alexus calling.

As soon as she answered, Alexus said, "How would you like to take over the family business?"

Chapter 6

Mary wanted to know Pedro's reason for their flight to Chicago but he wasn't talking.

Once they landed at O'Hare international airport they were whisked away in Pedro's armored white Hummer limousine, which was tailed by two red Range Rovers full of armed security.

He'd recently had the windows in the limo bulletproofed after Blake punched through one of them.

Mary —cute-faced and short-haired with a slender build, clad in a red Valentino dress over matching Louboutin sneakers— sat with her legs crossed and her eyes on Pedro. She had an attitude that he knew would remain until he told her what was going on.

Sadly, he couldn't tell her. She'd get even more upset.

He popped a bottle of Cristal champagne and offered her a glass.

"The Cristal guy is a racist," Mary said, and declined the glass.

"A lot of folks are racist. So what?" Pedro again reached out with the drink. "It's good champagne."

"Nothing's good that comes from a racist. Tell me why we're here. If you're gonna pull up somewhere and start shooting I want out of this limo right this second."

"I won't shoot." Pedro chuckled and glanced at the goldplated AK-47 that stood between his legs. It was equipped with a shell-catcher, a 100-round drum, and a red beam. "I only keep this thing around for protection. You know that. Don't I always keep it with me?"

"You're not telling me something, Pedro. I'm your lady now. It's common courtesy to tell your lady when you're getting ready to murder someone, just in case there's the slight chance that she wants absolutely nothing...to fucking...do with it."

Pedro gave Mary's attitude a wave of dismissal and drank the champagne for himself. His business was none of hers. She was well aware of his rank in the Costilla Cartel. She'd chosen to stick with him in spite of his cartel connections from the very beginning.

"I wanna go and visit my parents in Indianapolis. You can stay here and do whatever it is you wanna do," she said.

"Don't be foolish. Nothing's going to happen," Pedro assured, taking in a second swallow of the bubbly.

He wasn't certain that his words were the truth.

The last time he'd visited Chicago it had been to save Blake's life; this time it was to save the family business from the hands of a simple-minded young ghetto girl.

As soon as Alexus had phoned him with her decision to step down from the throne he'd packed his bags and got on the jet.

With her departure from the cartel, she was leaving Mercedes in charge, and Pedro was going to make damned sure that Mercedes turned down the offer and left the family business to him.

He raised his smartphone and dialed Mercedes's number as his driver pulled to the curb on the corner of Lake and Lockwood on Chicago's west side.

The redbrick apartment building on the corner was where Mercedes Costilla was born and raised with her drug-addicted mother, Whitney Clark.

Pedro reminisced about the night when Alexus ordered the cartel to murder a bunch of girls named Whitney in Michigan City, Indiana, all because Blake had allegedly cheated on her there with a girl named Whitney.

It was Pedro who'd killed two of the seven murdered Whitneys.

One of them was Whitney Clark, Mercedes and Porsche's mother.

"Hey, little cousin," he said with a modicum of excitement in his tone when Mercedes picked up.

"What do you want, Pedro?" Mercedes said.

"Alexus has stepped down. You're next in line, and then me. You'll turn it down, won't you?"

Mercedes hesitated. "I don't know," she said a few seconds later. "I might want that seat. I could run—"

"Didn't you buy that old building you were raised in? On the corner of Lake and Lockwood?"

"Yeah, I have a couple of friends running that corner now. Why?"

Pedro ended the call abruptly.

He noticed a group of four young black men with dreadlocks and thuggish demeanors standing around two black Escalades on big chrome rims across the street from the apartment building's front entrance. They all turned to his limousine and the two Range Rovers behind it, and their expressions shifted into scowls.

"Why are we here?" Mary asked.

"To send a message," Pedro replied quickly as he picked up the AK-47 and threw open his door.

The doors on the Rovers swung open at the same time.

Pedro opened fire on the four young men a second before his men began squeezing their triggers.

The scowling young thugs were gunned down to the cracked sidewalk within seconds.

King Rio

38

Chapter 7

Mercedes stared at her iPhone for several minutes, wondering what Pedro meant.

Nell and her sister Alycia had just arrived, and the surprise baby shower was under way.

All the girls —fourteen of them in all— were bunched around Nell as she opened the gifts and cried like a baby out of sheer gratefulness.

Instinctively, Mercedes went to the living room window and fingered down the blinds to look outside.

There was only a middle aged white woman jogging past with a poodle on a leash, and the mailman.

A moment later Porsche came over and joined her at the window.

"I sent the guys to the building to drop off some more dope," Mercedes said. "Alexus called me asking if I was interested in running the cartel. Then Pedro just called saying Alexus stepped down from her role as boss of the cartel. He asked me if I'd turn it down, I said I'd have to think about it, then he cut me off and asked about the building. He knows that I bought it. I said yeah, my guys run it, and he hung up."

"So?"

"I think he might do something to the guys. You know how little Pedro and Alexus care about the loss of lives."

"Well, call the guys," Porsche suggested.

Mercedes did just that, and she wasn't hugely surprised that her young soldiers didn't pick up.

She tried four more numbers and finally got an answer from Lavell, an 18-year-old 4CH who'd just recently come home from a yearlong bid in Stateville prison.

She cut on the speakerphone for Porsche's sake.

"Somebody pulled up in a white Hummer limo," Lavell said, sounding out of breath. "They had some red Range Rovers with em. Hopped out and chopped the lil homies down with them K's, whacked four of us before they sped off. We didn't even have a chance to shoot back."

Mercedes couldn't believe it. Her heart rate increased as she lowered the phone to her hip. Four of her men had just been gunned down in broad daylight, and there was no question who'd done it.

"Those motherfucking Mexicans," Porsche said in a disbelieving whisper. "Why would you tell him you had to think about it? Are you nuts? You should have told him to leave you out of it, dumbass. It's probably not even safe for us to stay here now."

"We'll be fine. Just...give me some time to think."

Mercedes put a finger between the blinds and separated them for a second look outside.

What she saw made her mouth fall open.

She gasped, and her eyes got big.

Hardly ten minutes had passed since the phone call from Pedro.

Parked at the curb out front was Pedro's white Hummer limousine, and two red Range Rovers were idling behind it.

Chapter 8
Four Weeks Later...

'...And in breaking couples news, Alexus Costilla and rapper Bulletface have rekindled their marriage. According to various sources, the Kings are spending time together with their children at the old Versace Mansion in Miami Beach. Alexus purchased the home three years ago for the hefty price of $145 million. Since then she's rumored to have spent another $40 million on renovations.

'With a combined net worth of $73.9 billion, they are America's highest paid couple. Bulletface raked in more cash last year than any other music artist, and his wife's television networks are bringing in big bucks from sponsors...'

The television was on E! News.

Lying back on Blake's chest in their oversized bed, Alexus was finally at peace. Blake had been right. Leaving the dope game when they did was a smart idea. The more Alexus thought about it the more she loved him for suggesting it. For the past month they'd been living happily in their spacious Miami Beach home without a care in the world.

Somehow, Pedro had gotten Mercedes to hand over leadership of the family business to him, and since then he'd been running the show from a newly renovated eighty-million-dollar mansion he bought for himself and his girlfriend in Matamoros.

Oddly, Alexus hadn't heard from Mercedes ever since the day she stopped running the cartel herself, though they had agreed to start talking more that very morning.

Alexus didn't mind not talking to her sister. She was content with Blake being faithful and spending all his time with her, and that's exactly what he was doing. Ever since the warehouse incident he'd severed ties with his side chicks, which was a fairly easy feat.

Neither girl wanted anything more to do with him.

Blake wrapped his arms around her waist and kissed the back of her neck.

"Doesn't this feel so perfect?" Alexus asked him. "Maybe this is God finally giving me my 'happily ever after'. That's all I really want, you know. All the money is nothing without love and family."

Blake's lips brushed across the nape of her neck. His hands caressed her thighs. She wore a tight pair of low-cut, white denim shorts and a white halter top. He had on just a black pair of Nike gym shorts and socks.

He had a bunch of white diamond jewelry on his nightstand next to his two iPhones and four boxes of cigarillos.

"It definitely feels good," Blake said. "Not having to worry about gettin' shot at every day. It's been a whole month of peace."

"The longest span of peace we've had." Alexus laughed once. "I can't believe how big the kids are getting. They're both growing up so fast."

"Know what else is growing up fast?"

"Spare me the details," Alexus said, knowing that nine times out of ten his mind was in the gutter.

"This dick."

"How'd I know you were going to say that?"

"Because you know how to keep it from growin'. You got the power to shrink it back down to size."

"I know how to cut it off, too."

"Get the fuck off me." He pushed her away, laughing, and she turned around and sat on his lap. "I'm dead muhfuckin serious, Alexus. Don't be saying no shit like that."

"Awww, my boo don't want his lil ding-ding cut off."

"Ain't shit little about my ding-ding."

He was rubbing all over her enormous derrière, grinning and biting his bottom lip the way he always did when he wanted to fuck her. She could see the hunger in his eyes.

"I don't know what it is about those gold teeth in your mouth that makes me so fucking horny." Alexus bit his bottom lip between her teeth. Her hands roamed his broad muscular chest and shoulders.

She felt his rapidly swelling 'ding-ding' pressing against the crotch of her shorts, and it made her want him even more. She'd been a lot more sexually active since the burns on her left leg and the stitches and staples in her left arm had begun to heal sooner than expected. Now that the pain was practically gone, she was enjoying herself more with her ridiculously handsome husband.

Blake was grateful for the positive shift in her health. He liked to do nothing more than fuck her brains out for most of the day. Alexus thought of the millions of women who constantly made it known that they wanted a man who could go all night long.

Alexus already had that man.

"I know why you like these golds," he said, and delivered a passionate kiss to her juicy lips. "You know how they feel rubbin' across that juicy."

"You wanna refresh my my mem—"

The sudden sound of a multiple light slaps at the bedroom door interrupted their moment.

Alexus sighed and shook her head. "King," she muttered discontentedly.

Their son King Neal was the only one who slapped on the door instead of knocking.

"Ma! Let me in this door."

The doorknob rattled.

Blake laughed. "What do you want, King?"

"I believe I said 'Ma', Daddy. I wasn't talking to you," was King's smart-mouthed reply.

Blake bit his lower lip, and Alexus knew that he was thinking of snatching their son up for the snide remark.

"Well," Alexus said, "what do you want?"

"My watch keeps falling off and I can't buckle it right."

"Tell your sister to help you."

"I did. She told me to get out her face. She got a ugly face, anyway. I don't wanna be in it."

Alexus was reluctant to pull herself away from Blake's hungry embrace; his cologne mixed with the air so perfectly that she wanted to stay in its space. He grabbed her by the waist and held her down as she started to get up.

"King!" Blake said, this time with the assertive tone of voice all fathers used to keep their children in line. "Go somewhere and sit down. We'll be out in a minute."

"No, let me clasp his watch, Blake. I won't even let him in," Alexus murmured.

Blake shook his head no.

Alexus couldn't help but to snicker. Her husband wanted her now and he wasn't going to let anyone get in the way of him getting her.

"Man, Daddy," King said and slapped the door once more. His gentle footfalls ensued as he ran from the door. Alexus heard something hit the floor in the hallway and knew he'd thrown the watch.

"If that boy doesn't act just like you," Alexus said, shaking her head and holding Blake's face in her hands. "You got him addicted to watches now."

"Shut up." Blake's hands went to the chest of her halter.

There was a sharp rip sound as he tore it right down the middle, exposing her bare breasts.

Alexus mashed a fingertip in his forehead for ripping the halter top off her, but then he sucked on a nipple and suddenly she didn't care about the shirt. The feel of his twirling tongue was overwhelming.

She stood up over him and peeled off her tight-fitting shorts. She had purposely not put on underwear after her morning bath, knowing that neither of them had any plans for the day outside of a planned outing this afternoon with the kids.

Blake sat forward with his head tilted back and put his mouth right up under her pussy as she applied her fingertips to her clitoris for a circular massage.

She inhaled sharply through her mouth as his tongue came back out to play, first dipping in between the lips and then swabbing around her fingertips, eager to push her over the edge with his clit-sucking maneuver.

She held him off for nearly a full minute before he was able to clamp his lips onto her clit.

Then it was over.

He sucked and swished saliva around the sensitive flesh, ramming first one finger and eventually two into her pussy as she moaned softly and gyrated her hips.

He began pumping his dick in a tight fist, while his other hand squeezed and caressed her meaty buttocks and pulled her closer.

Just one minute later, panting heavily and holding the back of his head, she said "Mm...I'm...I'm coming...I'm coming..."

Both of his strong veiny hands went to her ass. He kept sucking her clitoris as her pussy squirted like a water gun. The juices dripped down his chin and onto his powerfully muscled chest.

"Okay, stop, stop, stop, stop," Alexus said, pushing Blake's head away as she collapsed down onto the bed.

She landed on her hip and instinctively curled up into a fetal position as her legs shook and trembled involuntarily.

It was Blake's turn to stand over her.

"Come 'ere," he said, kicking off his shorts and boxers and staring down at her.

He was once again pumping his twelve-inch pole in his right hand. It was so fat and long that sometimes Alexus thought it might do some damage to her insides if he went too hard during one of their lovemaking sessions.

"You have to take it easy on me today," she said worriedly.

"I ain't gon' hurt you."

"I'm for real, Blake. I won't be able to walk straight. That shit hurts."

"I said I'll be gentle," he coaxed.

There was a drop of precum oozing out of the bulbous head. She stared at it until it began to dangle underneath the head, then she found the strength in her legs to get up on her knees and take his dick to the back of her throat.

She had gotten pretty good at deepthroating him. She was able to get the majority of his length in her throat and hold it there for twenty seconds at a time. Her record was twenty-seven seconds; she'd kept count on her smartphone the night of their honeymoon.

Blake wrapped her long, curly black hair around his fist and pounded his love muscle down her throat until she pulled back twenty seconds later. After a quick breath she took it back into her throat and went for another twenty, cupping and tugging at his scrotum while moving her tongue on the underside of his throbbing muscle. She wanted him to shoot off right down her throat. She didn't particularly care for the taste of semen but his thick loads were precious to her. She'd swallowed his seed too many times to count.

Unfortunately, Blake had other plans.

He took two steps back and dropped to his knees.

"Oh, Lordy," Alexus said with a giggle.

He pushed her back, got a good grip on her thighs, and dragged her to his brick-hard erection.

"Don't just jam it—" Alexus started.

She gasped as he jammed it right in, just what she'd been telling him not to do.

He pushed up her legs so that her knees were over her face and went to pounding.

She moaned with reckless abandon now, mouth wide open, eyes gaping, staring up at him as if he were some magical sex god rather than her husband. She reached up and clawed his chest, a part of her wanting to beg him to stop, the other part of her wishing he would drill her dripping-wet nookie forever.

"I love you," he said, parting her thighs and planting his lips against hers.

All she could do was moan. She tried to return the statement of love but couldn't. No words came out. She was experiencing too much painful pleasure.

Her body tensed and trembled and she moaned ecstatically as a second orgasm struck her. She dug her nails in his back, holding her breath. Her juices gushed out over his steadily thrusting pole.

He moved back and allowed her a moment to regain her composure before urging her to turn over.

Alexus knew Blake's favorite position. He loved to pull her hair and slap on her ass as he pounded her nookie from behind.

He did just that.

Holding on to her waist at first, he gave her the rapid strokes that he knew would drive her to a third orgasm in no time. Then he wrapped a fist in her hair and pulled her head back.

"Love you, baby," he said, pausing, his mouth an inch from her ear.

"Don't stop," Alexus said.

They were the only two words that came to mind.

Blake gave it to her roughly, slapping her ass and pulling her hair until his semen was dripping down onto their white Versace blanket, and even then he kept thrusting for another minute before finally stepping out of bed to get his black-and-gold Versace boxers.

"You're trying to get me pregnant again," Alexus said, completely out of breath as she lay flat on the bed and gazed at him. Her legs were trembling the way they always did when he finished putting it on her. "Look at my legs. They won't stop shaking."

"Come on, let's take a shower," he said. "We gotta get ready for this trip with the kids."

She stared after him as he went in the bathroom and turned on the shower.

As soon as she saw him step in the shower, her eyes flicked over to his two iPhones on the nightstand.

She had the burgeoning inclination to turn on the smartphones and investigate. Especially the one with the blinking notification light.

No, she told herself. I have to trust him. It's been a good thirty days so far, and I'm not about to go searching for trouble.

Though, in the back of her mind, she still was worried that he might cheat again.

She joined him in the shower and ogled his rich brown skin for a long moment as they scrubbed themselves clean, wondering if in the future she'd have to kill another bitch over what was hers.

Chapter 9

Going from being Atlanta's most popular stripper to being in the FBI's witness protection program wasn't easy for Tasia "Baddie Barbie" Olsen.

Instead of her newly renovated Buckhead home, she was living alone in a dreary two bedroom apartment in Tallahassee, Florida. Instead of her Bentley she was driving a used Honda Accord. Instead of twerking at Club Onyx and making anywhere between $1,500-$5,000 a night she was working evenings at Burger King. Instead of her identification cards reading Tasia Olsen, they now read Jasmine Winters.

Eagle's Point Townhomes was the exclusive housing provider of Tallahassee Community College, which was just another thing Tasia could add to the long list of complaints she had about her new living situation. The college kids were for the most part poor young men and women with little to do in their spare time other than drinking cheap liquor, smoking weed, popping pills, and having sex with each other. Tasia was confronted by the horny young men every time she she left the apartment, and with all the hips, thighs, and ass she possessed, she was cursed to receive catcalls and explicit details of exactly what a lot of the guys wanted to do to her.

Her new living conditions sucked, but it beat being in a casket.

"Something's better than nothing," she mumbled to herself as she set up her ironing board next to the coffee table in her cramped living room.

As bad as she wanted to go back to the A she knew that it wouldn't be the wisest thing to do with the Mexican Mafia on her trail.

"I should've told the feds about Alexus Costilla's involvement. Bitch thinks she runs the fucking world. Well, all that money didn't stop me from fucking your man, now, did it?"

She started ironing her uniform and watching the local news. A 14-year-old girl had gone missing, and there was an Amber alert for her. Peaceful demonstrators were outside the police department's headquarters protesting over the death of an 18-year-old

Black man who'd been shot and killed by police last night after being pulled over for speeding.

Tasia shook her head at the news. She hated it when Black men were murdered by police. She'd lost a friend in middle school to a White policeman's gun. Daniel Murphy was just fourteen when he was shot twice in the back after running from an NYPD officer who'd tried to stop him for a pat-down.

The next news story drastically changed her mood.

Alexus had recently spent $684 million on a customized Boeing 747 jet for her husband, and abc27 News had exclusive photos of the plane's lavish interior. There were bedrooms and lounges, flat screen televisions and white leather furniture.

It was enough to make Tasia scream, which she did, just as someone knocked on her front door.

"Jasmine? Girl, you okay in there?"

It was Tasha, the heavyset Jamaican woman from across the hall. Tasha's sister, Ebanee, worked with Tasia at Burger King. They were under the impression that Tasia was Jasmine from Miami, a girl who'd fled from an abusive relationship with an alcoholic fiancé named Tommy.

Tasia went to the door and opened it wearing a fake smile.

"What are you in here hollering about?" Tasha asked as she stepped inside and looked around. "That nigga ain't came back and found you, has he? 'Cause I got my gun. Won't be no ass whoopin' in here unless it's us doing the whoopin'."

"I'm not worried about that nigga. Have a seat. Want somethin' to drink?"

Tasha said yes, she'd appreciate a soda. Ebanee was on her way over in a few minutes, she was getting her hair together.

Lucky for Tasha there was a 20-ounce Mountain Dew in the fridge that Tasia had gotten last night from the 7/11 down the street. She brought it to Tasha, then went back to ironing her pants.

"What in the world were you hollering for?" Tasha asked.

"Just stressing. I don't like working. I'm thinking about quitting already. It's not enough money for me."

"That asshole you were with must have had good money."

"Yeah, he had it all." Tasia was talking about Blake, though she knew Tasha was thinking of the abusive, imaginary ex. "He bought me everything I ever wanted. I was always his side chick, though. He had a wife he'd been separated from for a while. Things took a turn for the worse when she came back in the picture. She's just as fucked up mentally as he is. I hate both of their asses."

"Know what I say? Fuck him and that skank bitch. Live your life. Start over and find real love this time. You're young and beautiful, you got one of those big ol' butts like the strippers have, and you got class 'cause I ain't heard about you messing with none of these triflin' ass niggas in this apartment complex."

"That'll never happen."

"I don't know, now. Don't speak so soon. There are a couple of handsomes in the group. Drex in the next building over— he doesn't look too bad. He's got that nice car. And you see the way he looks at you. He's asked for your number a hundred times already."

"He can ask a hundred more times. Hell, a thousand. I don't care. I'll be single forever before I even think about givin' some pussy to one of these niggas."

Tasia wasn't being completely honest. She'd actual thought about doing a lot more than just giving Drex some pussy. He was tall and dark, practically all muscle, and he always smelled good and looked fresh. He worked part time as a physical trainer at Planet Fitness. Tasia knew this from Ebanee, who was secretly cheating on her boyfriend of two years with a cousin of Drex's.

"Let that nigga look at me the way he looks at you," Tasha said. "Just one damn time is all it's gon' take. I'll ride that nigga like his last bitch should've."

Tasia laughed and shook her head. "Find you something to watch on that TV. Please. I am not tryna hear your sex fantasies."

It never took Tasha long to find a channel to talk about. This time it was Jerry Springer. 'I Slept With Your Brother and the Baby Might Be His' was the caption at the bottom of the screen.

Ebanee walked in a few minutes later, already dressed for work and chewing on a piece of gum. She was buxom and pretty, dark like her sister and a hundred pounds lighter. Gold rings decorated her every finger, and on her neck she wore four thin gold necklaces.

"Why are you not dressed?" Ebanee asked.

"Because I really don't wanna go to work," Tasia said as she started on her shirt. She was perfectly fine with not going in at all and spending her afternoon watching movies in the sweatpants and T-shirt she had on now.

There was really no need for the job. The $180,000 she had hidden inside the brown leather sofa Tasha was sitting on was more than enough for her to live without employment for a long time, but she thought being stuck in the small apartment 24/7 was worse than flipping burgers.

Her hair was black now, unlike her usual colorful weaves. The diamond jewelry she used to wear was all hidden away in a box at her bank. Her Bentley was at her sister Fantasia's house in Decatur, Georgia, along with the majority of her clothes and personal belongings. She'd gone from having a closet full of expensive dresses and heels to just five pairs of Nikes and a bunch of sweats, jeans, and shirts.

Her sister had been released from the hospital in Atlanta two weeks ago. Fantasia was shot during one of the Mexican Mafia's attempts on her life.

Tasia got dressed right in front of Tasha and Ebanee, because she feared one of them might go snooping around in the sofa if she left them alone for too long.

Tasha went back to her apartment across the hall as Tasia and Ebanee left out for work.

Not surprisingly, a dozen young men were standing around in the parking lot, thirstily anticipating Tasia's departure just so they could see her.

Ebanee's black Mercury Mountaineer was the vehicle of choice.

As soon as Ebanee started the engine she said, "You are not going to believe what everybody at school was talking about today."

"If you have those lil boys—"

"Nope, it wasn't me. They've all been sharing this video somebody recorded of you the other night. Here" —she handed her smartphone to Tasia— "hit my Facebook app. It's on my page. Don't ask me why they tagged me in it."

A video? Tasia wondered who had recorded her 'the other night'. The only embarrassing thing she could think of doing at night was cramming herself to orgasm every night with her dildo.

When she saw the video she knew who'd recorded it.

The words over the picture read: 'Look at all dat gotdamn dats Eb's friend from Burger King.' The sentence was followed by a bunch of cake emojis.

It was a 27-second video of her getting out of her car and walking to her apartment. She'd just returned from a trip to 7/11 for nachos, candy, and the Mountain Dew she'd just given to Tasha.

Tasia instantly knew that it was all about her butt. She'd worn a pair of white leggings without any underwear. Her ass shook with every step she took.

She remembered seeing Drex standing out front with some other men when she pulled up that night.

"One of Drex's punk ass friends did this bullshit. Wait til I see his black ass again," Tasia said, her face twisted in anger.

"It ain't a bad thing, Jasmine. Do you know how many bitches wish they had ass like that? Everybody just wanted to know your name, that's all. You never talk to anybody."

"I'm antisocial, okay? Please do me a favor and tell your little college friends not to record videos of my ass like some kind of perverted freaks. That is just weird. I feel violated."

"Drex has a crush on you, Jasmine. Every girl in school knows it, too. You should talk to him. Give him a chance."

Tasia rolled her eyes and changed the subject. "Did you see the news about Alexus Costilla buying—"

"The plane for Bulletface," Ebanee said, nodding her head as she drove out of the parking lot. "Yeah, I saw it. I actually have a story about me and him. People never believe me when I tell them that I used to mess around with Bulletface."

Tasia's expression turned sour. She'd never heard Eb mention Blake, but then again they'd never spoken about him. He was a part of her life that had to remain a secret.

"Yeah-the-fuck-right," Tasia said. "You ain't never fucked with Bulletface."

"I swear on my momma's grave I did. He took me to this nice hotel in Miami Beach once, and we fucked all night long."

"Excuse me for not believing you."

"Did I ask you to believe me? I'm telling you the truth, I don't care if you believe me or not. I fucked with him a couple of times. He gave me some bands but I blew the shit, thinking we'd still be fucking around for a while, but he dropped me like a bad habit." Eb laughed and shook her head as she halted at a red light. She glanced over at Tasia. "One of the girls at school said you look like that stripper Bulletface was messing around with when Alexus was in the hospital. The pictures of the girl on MediaTakeout.com look almost exactly like you, I mean ass and all, it's crazy. All you have to do is put on some makeup and dye your hair pink and you'd be her twin."

Tasia almost wanted to come straight out and tell Ebanee who she really was, if for no other reason than to make Eb recant the lie she'd just told about sleeping with Blake.

Then again, the way Blake was, there was no telling if he'd fucked Ebanee or not. After all, he'd been married when Tasia started fucking him.

"I got pictures of me and Blake in the hotel room," Eb said, and suddenly Tasia believed her. "Go to the sent messages in my email. I starred all of em before I sent em to him."

As bad as Tasia wanted Ebanee to be joking she had a feeling that she wasn't being led on, and when she touched the Gmail icon on Eb's smartphone and went to the sent emails she found herself stunned by the truth.

There were four pictures of Blake and Ebanee hugging in front of a mirror. His hands were all over her ass in every pic.

Tasia's nostrils flared as she struggled to keep her rage in check.

"See?" Eb said, beaming. "You thought I was lying, didn't you? I never really show off those pictures. Only a few people have seen em."

"You ever get his phone number?" Tasia asked.

Ebanee nodded her head yes. "He's changed it since then. I'm not trying to reach him anyway. He's married now. I'm trying to find me a boss nigga like him that'll wife me up. We need to start goin' out to the club or somethin'. You'd be surprised at how many pro athletes go out partying at the nightclubs around here every night."

Tasia declined the offer. She didn't wanna go out to meet anyone.

Well, maybe she'd take another night with Blake...

Chapter 10

'Bulletface...Bad Guy

Throwin' money bags in the damn sky

MBM, we so damn fly

And it's Money Bagz til I damn die

Choppa wit' me at all times

Sold kilograms, sold hards dimes

Got a bad bitch, put a ring on it

And every bitch in her squad dimes

Just got me a new jet

Cost about seven hun'ed mill

Got a K and seven hun'ed round drums

Don't make me catch seven hun'ed kills

Niggas couldn't get rich as me if they went and signed seven hun'ed deals

Hit Adrianna's wit a Brinks truck, throwin all hun'eds my money real

Most you niggas ain't from the field, don't even know how dem choppas feel

I sold crack, been shot for real, niggas disappeared, David Copperfield

Yo bitch want me to cop a feel

I came from where no cops could chill

I came from where no opps could chill

Bitch, I'm from the block for real

My son blessed...King shit

Neal shit, big T shit

Nigga, we da shit

Nigga don't like it, tell his baby momma she can eat a dick

Disrespect and he gon eat a clip

I got thirty shots for dat nigga

Couple years ago I was big bankin', and now my money got bigga

But I'm still the same lil nigga who was on the Dub totin' that pistol

If you think I changed come try me, nigga, and I bet I give you yo issue...'

Ever since Alexus had one of the nine bedrooms in The Versace Mansion converted into a high-tech recording studio, Blake had been making a lot of his music here in Miami Beach. He enjoyed being here more than their many other homes because it was a warm place where celebrities weren't hounded as much as they were in more populated cities. There were far too many music and sports superstars who visited the area year-round. Several times over the past few weeks Blake and Alexus had ventured out in the white Bugatti Veyron Grand Sport she'd had flown here for whenever they wanted to go out for a drive. They'd shopped on Collins Avenue and even attended one of Diddy's parties down the street at the Fontainebleau. The paparazzi had hounded them, but it had been fairly easy for them to return home without interference.

He was standing at the mic in the recording booth, staring through the glass at Alexus and his crew of music engineers as he worked on a new mixtape he would be dropping in the coming weeks. It was good being with Alexus all day and night but the streets were asking for another selection of hits for the summer, and as a multiplatinum rap artist he felt obligated to give the fans what they asked for.

Alexus gave him a round of applause when he stepped out of the booth after freestyling seven whole songs straight.

"You are the king for a reason," she said, smiling widely. "I can't wait for all of that to drop."

"Me neither. Come on." He held her hand and stepped out in the hallway while his music crew mixed and mastered the tracks. They went down the staircase hand in hand.

Savaria and King Neal were in the foyer playing, just as they always did while he recorded. Vari was laughing and running from King's shiny silver miniature Ferrari as he tried his best to run her over with it.

"King," Alexus said, "if you hurt her I'm hurting you."

"Leave my lil nigga alone." Blake's hands roamed across his wife's bountiful buttocks, and he kissed her lips.

"There's something I meant to tell you about your little girl-friend," Alexus said. "That bitch named Barbie."

"Yeah?" Blake hoped it wasn't news of Barbie's murder.

"She was plotting on you the whole time you and her were together. That's the other Tasia's sister. The one who used to be with Cereniti. The one you shot in the face in—"

"I ain't shot nobody."

"Well, whatever. Barbie wanted to set you up to get clapped for that shit. You're lucky I ran that bitch off when I did."

"I ain't worried 'bout nothin'. Fuck her. I'm focused on this mixtape. I ain't featuring nobody but Hove and Wayne on it. That's it. The greatest of the greats. And I'm gon' kill every track."

"How do you memorize all that stuff?" Alexus asked, gazing up at him. "I used to think all those rappers lied about freestyling their songs."

She was on her tippy toes in pair of white fur slippers. She wore white sweatpants and a Bulletface T-shirt. Blake had put his gym shorts back on, along with a plain white tee and a gold Rolex watch.

"I don't do no lying."

"Yeah, unless it's about one of those bitches."

"Stop bringin' that shit up."

She rolled her eyes and spun away from him. "Whatever. I'm about to get dressed."

Blake gazed lustfully at his wife's generous curves as she headed off to their bedroom. The way her ass wobbled as she walked was enough to drive any man wild.

His attention went to the kids, and he laughed as Vari jumped over the mini Ferrari just before King could hit her.

The notification light began blinking on Blake's iPhone. He checked it and saw that he had a new email.

It was from a girl he had slept with a couple of times when he and Alexus had briefly separated a few years ago.

The girl's name was Ebanee.

Blake briefly contemplated deleting the message without reading it. He had his mind set on being faithful to Alexus and raising his children righteously.

Besides, there was no way he would cheat on his wife now. Not after she'd sent one of his side pieces running to a witness protection program and hung another upside down by a length of chain in an abandoned warehouse. He wasn't trying to get anyone else kidnapped or murdered. Being faithful was saving lives.

Watching the kids play, he reminisced about the few times he'd spent with Ebanee and decided he would just read the email and never reply.

The message made his eyebrows lift up in surprise.

'It's Barb. Call me, please. 404-555-2212. I get off work at 10:00 tonight. And don't ask how I met Eb and was able to message you from her email. Long story.'

Blake's mouth was left hanging open after reading the message.

Barb was Tasia "Baddie Barbie" Olsen.

How in the fuck had she managed to meet one of his exes and access his email?

He thought back to the night he had Ebanee send some photos they'd taken together to his email and knew it must be how Eb's email was linked to his.

But the question remained: How did Barbie meet Ebanee?

Was there something to the two of them crossing paths or was it a mere coincidence?

He thought it over as he joined Alexus in the bedroom and changed into an all white Balmain shirt-and-jeans outfit with a fresh white pair of Louboutin sneakers. He added five white diamond necklaces, a chunky white diamond bracelet, his custom made white diamond Hublot watch, and a white Louis Vuitton belt with white diamonds in the LV logo. A dash of cologne later he was ready to go but still not ready to make a decision on whether or not he'd phone Barbie later tonight.

By the time Alexus came out of the bathroom, dressed comfortably in a snug-fitting white Chanel dress over matching six-inch Louboutin heels, Blake had two blunts rolled on his nightstand and was pouring Promethazine with Codeine out of a pint-sized medicine bottle into his double-stacked Styrofoam cup of Sprite on ice.

He looked at her and grinned his signature grin.

Like his, her neck and wrists were also aglow with large white diamonds. She had a white leather Chanel shoulder bag under one arm and a matching duffle bag in her other hand. Her sparkling green eyes studied him closely.

"I hope you don't get me pregnant again any time soon," she said as she walked to him and kissed him on the cheek. "All that Lean and Kush in your system might make our baby slow or something."

"Make him a young player." Blake tasted the Lean and nodded his head in agreement with the taste.

"A special Olympics player," Alexus countered.

Blake chuckled. He put a blunt behind his ear and lit the other one. "You ready to go?"

"You're not smoking in front of the kids."

"Y'all take the Sprinter. I'll drive the Bugatti."

"It's a family outing, Blake. I want you to enjoy it with us."

Blake picked up his own white duffle bag — a Louis Vuitton — and opened the bedroom door. "I'm smokin' my weed either while we're on the way there or right now."

"Jerk."

"Slurp," Blake replied.

Laughing heartily, Alexus slapped him on the shoulder. "Asshole, stop telling me that. That's so disrespectful."

"What, slurp? What's so disrespectful about it? You slurp, don't you?"

"Yeah, just like you slurp on this pussy."

"Okay, then. I ain't denying that." Blake walked out like he'd proven his point and there was nothing more to say, grinning widely as Alexus strutted along behind him.

She took King and Vari to their bedrooms to pack up the things they'd need while Blake went out the side door to the outside patio and smoked his blunt while lying back on a white chaise lounge and staring up into the clear blue sky.

It was 91 degrees in Miami Beach, Florida. The palm trees were swaying and there was hardly a breeze. The weed took Blake to a sea of thoughts, the first of which was Baddie Barbie.

He wouldn't call her. There was no need to. He had told her from the beginning that he wasn't into having a relationship. It was strictly sex and good times. When he learned that Barbie was related to Jantasia Olsen he'd thrown her into a mirror and left her with staples in the back of her head. Then, feeling bad afterward and try-ing to keep her from pressing charges, he had paid her $100,000 in cash and later purchased her a quarter-million-dollar pink Bentley coupe. He had kept her around for more fun and then ditched her after a suspicious incident where Barbie and her friend had seem-ingly lured him into a shootout with a deadly street gang in Chicago.

Yeah, he definitely wasn't going to call her.

He thought of the beef he had with a rich Chicago mobster named Cup. It was a beef that had been initiated by Mercedes Costilla. He knew it for a fact. Mercedes sent a team of young gang members to shoot up Cup's nightclubs while shouting out the name of Blake's record label. Blake knew that Mercedes was only setting him up for a war with Cup and the Traveling Vice Lords, the gang that Cup ran with an iron fist.

Blake's old mentor Lil Lord was an original member of the TVL's. When Lil Lord was sentenced to thirty five years for a mur-der in Blake's hometown of Michigan City, Indiana, Blake and Cup's business relationship had turned sour. Cup and his gang had ended up kidnapping Savaria and slitting her mom's throat, but not before making off with $50 million in ransom money. Alexus's family had convinced Blake to end his beef with Cup in order to bring in the drug money from Chicago's west side streets, and Blake had reluctantly agreed.

Now, though, Blake didn't mind dealing with Cup in the same way that Cup had dealt with Savaria's mom. After all, Ashley Joy had been Blake's first love, the mother of his first child. Maybe the time was ripe to avenge her death.

Blake's phone rang just then.

It was a call from Young Meach, one of his recording artists and longtime friends.

"Bruh, where you at? Still in Miami?" Meach asked.

"Yeah," Blake said. "Why, what's the thought?"

"We got this show in Chicago tonight. Just wonderin' if you talked to Cup yet or if we gotta be on that when we get there."

"Bring the goons out. Fuck it, if niggas wanna take it there we can get straight to gunplay. Hope they don't think I'm retired or somethin' 'cause I'm laid up wit' wifey. I'll still slide on a muhfucka."

"I'm just tellin' you what's up before we get there. We just landed at Midway. I'm gon' hit Young when I get off the line with you and have him bring everybody."

"Bring all the guns, too," Blake said, blowing perfect circles of Kush smoke in the air. "Straight thirty rounds or better. Wet a muhfucka clean up if need be. I don't know if niggas think it's some hoes in MBM Gang but they can find out quick. Ain't shit sweet. We're bosses. We will be tested. But those who test us will fail every time. We got all the money on our side. Drop fifty bands on one of the lil niggas and send em his way if he on that. I should smoke that nigga anyway for killin' Ashley."

"You know I'm on whatever you on, bruh. Biggs, Mocha, and Scrill here with me. We got that big ass concert tonight at Wrigley Field. That hoe sold out, too. You should fly up here and surprise the fans wit' a performance. You know they're missin' you."

"Y'all can handle that shit. I'm wit' wifey and the kids today."

"A'ight, I'll dolla atchoo later, the bad way."

"DBG, MBM," Blake said, meaning Dem Bad Guyz, Money Bagz Management.

He pressed end and sat up for another sip of Lean. The blunt was practically gone, so he hit it once more and dropped the roach in the ashtray next to his chair. He'd save the second blunt for later.

The kids were certain to get on his nerves before the trip was over. He'd need the Kush blunt.

He cut the idea of him driving alone in the Bugatti and joined Alexus and the kids in the Sprinter van. Now they had four legitimate bodyguards who were professional bodybuilders instead of experienced cartel thugs. The strong men put away the luggage and two coolers full of sandwiches and sodas and then followed behind the Sprinter in a white Escalade on big white Forgiato rims.

Remo, an older guy who Blake had become acquainted with during several visits to his hometown's county jail, was their driver. Remo's skin was as dark as the night, and his hair was wavy and just as black with sprinkles of gray. He'd been shot in the shoulder a few months ago but now he seemed to be doing much better.

"Daddy," King asked, "where you taking us to at this time of day?"

Blake chuckled and leaned forward to rub his little man's head.

"The Miami Children's Museum," Blake said. "It'll be fun."

Chapter 11

Pedro Costilla had scared Mercedes away from her position as boss of The Costilla Cartel when he murdered four of her men on the corner of Lake and Lockwood.

Today Mercedes wasn't afraid.

She and nearly fifty others were on the very same corner where the murders had taken place, each of them wearing white T-shirts with pictures of the slain young men along with gang signs that indicated the mob's allegiance to the 4 Corner Hustlers.

A $200,000 donation to the mob had gotten Mercedes the rank of 5-star Universal Elite for the organization, the highest rank attainable.

Though most of the money had gone to the mob's bosses that were now in prison, some of it had gone to the gang on the street, and Mercedes had spent $1 million more to put most of the young guys in new-model Cadillacs and Chevys on big chrome rims and to keep thick bankrolls in their pockets.

She'd made up her mind that she would do whatever was needed to build up her gang's defenses against the threats they faced every day. The guns on most of their hips had come from her. So had the thirty-round extended clips and fifty-round drums.

Mercedes wasn't taking any more chances.

Porsche and Sasha were now full-blown lesbians, or at least that's how they acted in front of everyone. It was becoming all too regular for Mercedes to twist her face in disgust as she watched the girl and her sister French kissing and fondling one another in public.

They were doing it now, leaning across the center console in Porsche's Maybach with the doors wide open for all to see while Mercedes stood nearby eating from a plate of barbecued ribs, macaroni and cheese, and potato salad with Shakema at her side.

"Who would've ever thought that Porsche was a dyke this whole time," Shakema muttered thoughtfully.

"She's just run out of dicks to suck," Mercedes said.

Porsche had definitely gotten around in the neighborhood before Mercedes ran into the wealth of her father's family. In their

65

poorer days, Mercedes had resorted to tricking with older men for money to pay the bills, while Porsche had partied and had sex with just about every one of the gang members who were now standing around enjoying the barbecue with them.

Mercedes had paid for the food. It was a block party. There were two barbeque grills going. Half the neighborhood was outside in the warm weather with her, gratefully accepting the free food and drinks. A few girls and one cowardly man had voiced their worries over an ongoing beef the guys on the block had with a clique of Conservative Vice Lords down the street but Mercedes didn't care. One of the black Escalades Mercedes bought for her crew was blasting out a Chief Keef song; the young gang members were charged up because of it. Mercedes could tell that they were ready to shoot at any opposition who happened to pass by.

"What happened to the TV show?" Shakema asked.

Mercedes gave a shrug. "I never called the bitch back. Who knows, she might've sent Pedro to do that shit. You never know with them." She'd told Shakema everything about what had transpired between her and Pedro before the shooting.

"You need to send some of these young niggas at those Mexicans. You know I grew up with Archie. They killed that man right here on this corner, Mercedes. And for what? Because of some Mexican drug cartel he had nothing to do with? That's sad. That motherfucker Pedro needs to pay for what he did. I hope one of those other cartels catch his ass slippin' in Mexico and do him the same damn way."

"Me, too. It's cool, though. Let him bring his ass through here on that bullshit again. You better believe we're ready now. He won't make it past this corner." Mercedes dumped a forkful of macaroni in her mouth and chewed. "I'm thinking about calling Alexus and telling her I wanna be the boss. I think they'll have to give it to me."

"Are you ready for something as big as that? I bet it takes a lot to run that kind of business. Those guys are heartless, Mercedes. I saw on the internet once where one of those cartels cut off a man's head with a chainsaw, then they cut off another man's head with a tiny little knife. Jesus, I would hate to die like that. I hope you don't have to get involved in that kind of evil stuff."

Mercedes had seen worse during a trip to Mexico with Alexus a while back. The Costilla Cartel had executed and beheaded over a hundred men and women right in front of Mercedes, and on Alexus's orders, at that.

"We're from Chicago," Mercedes reminded her unattractive friend. "I'll shoot a nigga all day, but I'm not cutting off no heads. Other than that I'm more than ready to run the cartel."

Shakema shook her head. "I don't think so. Hell, you don't even know a word of Spanish. You should just work with them if anything. I know they got kilos of dope. Get some of that shit and dump it on the squad. Let these lil niggas ball, and you can sit back and reap the benefits. A couple of kilos is all it'll take."

"I'll get more than a couple."

"You should call Alexus. I know you barely know her but she's your blood sister and she's a goddamn billionaire. You got long money now but it can't hurt to get more."

Mercedes looked at the teddy bears and roses that were piled high beside the light pole on the corner where four of her men had taken their last breaths.

"I really wanna do somethin' to them, Kema. My guys aren't going to be the only dead bodies around here."

"Play your cards right."

"Oh, I will." Mercedes was talking to herself more than she was to Shakema.

She finished eating and then went to her shiny black Maybach and got in the back seat...just as a raggedy blue Altima came speeding down Lake.

There was a young black teenage boy hanging out the rear driver's side window with a gun in his hand.

"Watch out, joe!" someone shouted just as the boy opened fire.

He got off three or four shots before Mercedes's heavily armed young gangsters let him have it.

She watched it all from her backseat. The boy took so many shots to the head and body that he was knocked back into the car as the driver turned away from the gang and attempted to speed off up Lockwood.

The 4 Corner Hustlers kept shooting until the car swerved and crashed into an old brown van.

Marko, one of Mercedes's most trusted young hitters, ran up to the car and emptied an entire thirty-round clip into its driver's side doors.

As Shakema was racing away, followed closely by Porsche, Mercedes said, "Shit like that will happen every time a nigga slides on my people. Let Pedro bring his ass through here again."

"I think that shit right there might have just started a war with the CVL's, Mercedes. I saw them driving around in that car a couple of—"

"I could care less who it starts a war with. Evidently it was already war if that nigga thought he could come through shooting like that. Fuck them."

Mercedes was in her element. The Costilla Cartel was supposed to be hers, but now it didn't matter because she was the head of a Chicago street gang that was just as violent as her family's cartel. She would sit here in Chicago and build her own empire...until her organization was strong enough to do some serious damage to her cousin Pedro Costilla and his men.

Chapter 12

The trip to the children's museum was abruptly canceled when King Neal set his eyes on Jungle Island, which was directly across the street from the museum.

At a quarter past noon Blake found himself irritating Alexus at the penguin exhibit while the kids gawked at the portly little snow birds.

"Blake, if you pinch my ass again I'm slapping you right in front of all these people," Alexus warned.

Just about every man and woman in the building had their smartphones trained on the celebrity couple, but Alexus was doing her best to focus on the kids.

"It's called PDA," Blake said with a chuckle. "Public display of affection."

"I'll give your ass some affection, alright." Alexus gave him a serious look, and he backed off.

They moved along to the tortoise exhibit. Savaria fell in love with the large turtles at first sight.

"Daddy, can I have a turtle?" she asked.

"Hell no," Blake replied quickly.

"You never let me have anything," Vari complained. She turned and asked Alexus instead.

Alexus smiled at Blake. To Savaria she said, "We'll go out and get you a turtle tomorrow."

The look on Blake's face said it all. He wanted to argue over the pet turtle but now wasn't the time.

"Thank you, Ma." Vari hugged Alexus and went back to ogling the tortoises.

What Alexus wanted to see most was the lions, and it took them an hour of walking along trails and seeing other exotic animals — flamingos, baboons, kangaroos, warthogs, and all kinds of birds and reptiles — before they finally made it to the lions and tigers.

Alexus took over a hundred pictures of the animals in between signing autographs and taking pics with random people who were more excited to see her and "Bulletface" than they were to see the animals.

They ended up at a playground, and the kids took off running to play while Blake and Alexus sat down at a picnic table and ate a couple of sandwiches.

"I swear," Blake said, biting into a chicken sandwich, "this famous shit ain't for me no more. I hate this shit. A nigga can't even eat a sandwich in peace." He glanced at a group of parents who were recording video and snapping photos of him and Alexus from the next table over. "They act like they ain't never seen a rich nigga before."

"Maybe they haven't," Alexus reasoned.

She watched Blake as he ate, hardly even touching her own sandwich. It felt so good to be spending time with her husband. Looking at him, she could understand why girls were wild for the rap legend they called Bulletface. He was so fine, tall, and dark. He was rich, though nowhere near as wealthy as her. He was strongly built and always smelled like he'd just gotten out of the bathtub. Men like him were rare, like an endangered species, so it was completely understandable why women chased after him the way they did. She couldn't blame them. Especially with the way he put it down in the bedroom. Blake King was definitely a keeper, and Alexus knew that she'd do anything in her power to keep him.

One thing that she would not go for was him cheating on her again.

So far, though, he was putting out all the right vibes. He'd promised to remain faithful to her, and that's all she wanted.

She cracked open a can of orange Crush soda and dropped a straw in the hole.

"My lil niggas on the way to Chicago," Blake said when he was done with his sandwich. "That situation with Cup needs to get tended to immediately. I told Meach to bring out the choppas and handle whatever comes his way."

"You should've had that man killed a long time ago," Alexus said. "I tried to do it myself. He's lucky he had on a vest. I'd have shot him in the face if we weren't in my limo at the time. You know how much I used to love that Rolls-Royce limousine."

"I know." Blake took the can from her and drank from the straw. "I'm about to end this shit for good this time around. Fuck all this playin' around. I'm done with the beefs and arguments with these niggas. From now on it's cemeteries."

"Don't drink all my soda."

"Get another one."

"How about you get your own? Black ass bastard." She reached for the ice-cold can, and he leaned away from her and drank until no more soda flowed through the straw.

"Here you go." He grinned and pushed the can at her.

"Can't stand your black ass," Alexus muttered as she signaled for a bodyguard to hand her another soda.

Just then, her iPhone lit up with a call from Enrique, who'd been staying in Mexico with Pedro and the rest of the Costilla Cartel.

"When are you coming back?" He spoke in Spanish "You know how badly we need you here. Pedro's doing okay but this is your business."

"I'm not coming back. I'm perfectly content with the life I'm living now."

"Yeah, until he cheats on you again. Then what?"

"That's not going to happen again. We're doing much, much better now, Enrique. Don't worry about me."

There was a brief pause. Blake stared at her, no doubt wondering what Enrique was calling about.

"We've found Gamuza again. This time he's all ours," Enrique said finally.

Gamuza was the boss of the Los Zetas Cartel, the man who'd beheaded Alexus's grandfather long before she was ever born. She'd been on the hunt for him ever since her grandmother passed away and left her in charge of the Costilla Cartel.

Enrique knew how badly she wanted Gamuza's head.

"Where is he?" she asked

"In Cancun. He's been staying in a compound near the resort. This time we actually have a girl in the room with him. There won't be any tunnels for him to escape through."

Alexus took a deep breath. Her eyes followed Blake as he walked over and joined the kids at the slide.

"I'm in," she said, unable to resist the opportunity to do what her father had wanted done to Gamuza. "But I'm not stepping foot on my jet until you have him in your custody. Call me when you have him. I wanna do the deed."

"Sure thing."

Alexus set the smartphone down and cracked open another soda. She would enjoy her day with the family without thinking about Gamuza and the Los Zetas, and when the time came to murder Gamuza, she would do it with no hesitation.

Chapter 13

A strongly bubbling Jacuzzi, a bottle of Ace of Spades champagne, and his stunningly attractive girlfriend — Mary, a 21-year-old Black woman from Indianapolis who'd been a college student out of El Paso, Texas when he met her at a bar in Juarez, Mexico — was all Pedro Costilla needed to settle into another sizzling-hot day at the Costilla vacation resort in Cancun, Mexico.

"Here," he said, pouring some champagne in a crystal stem glass for Mary as she sat beside him in the steaming water, wearing a two-piece Gucci bikini, her neck, ears, fingers, and wrists shining with over $1 million worth of large yellow diamonds. "It's Jay Z's champagne, you can drink this."

"I know whose champagne it is," Mary said, accepting the glass. Months earlier she'd had a dispute with him over a glass of Cristal champagne, insisting that she would never drink the beverage as long as she lived because the CEO of the champagne company was racist toward Blacks.

The Jacuzzi was right at the window of their 40th-floor penthouse suite. It overlooked the resort's water park, and it was one of Pedro's favorite spots in all of Mexico. Knowing that the resort was built off the dirty money he and the rest of the Costillas had made trafficking thousands of kilos of cocaine into the United States gave Pedro a deserving feeling. The Costilla Cartel's billions was responsible for this wonderful paradise, and Pedro had played a major part in its success.

The warm, churning water also served another purpose: it helped ease his worries over his cousin Alexus's return to Mexico.

He was concerned that maybe she would want to be in charge again after she got a glimpse of him running things.

"You're worried about something," Mary guessed correctly. "What is it?"

"It's nothing." Pedro drank from the bottle. "I just don't know about Alexus coming here to take out that fucking Gamuza. I feel like it's something I should do. She's not the boss anymore. I'm the boss, you know? I don't know why Enrique would tell her to fly in for Gamuza. That's just asking for her to take over."

"Would you have to give up control of the business if she wanted her spot back?" Mary gave him a tender kiss on the shoulder, an inch to the side of the strap that held his white leather shoulder holster in place.

He had a goldplated .50-caliber Desert Eagle pistol in the holster.

"It's the way things go," Pedro said with a nod. "She's the top boss as long as she's alive. Sure, she can pass it on to us but this will always be her cartel."

"Maybe she needs to stop being alive."

"Don't say that."

"I'm just saying...in the movies, and in real life with those Italian mobsters who came to America, it wasn't rare for a boss to be killed so another could take over. You see how dumb she is about Bulletface. You don't want someone like her running a drug cartel. She won't think clearly. She'll be acting off emotion. She'll be chasing after Bulletface instead of being a boss. Look at how you've changed things for the good. The Feds were all over you guys when she was here. Most of your family was killed when Alexus was boss. I think you'd be dumb not to have something done to her if she comes here with the mind to run the cartel."

"I'm not going to have my little cousin killed." Pedro was shaking his head. "No matter what she does I'll love and protect her until the very end."

"You're a dumbass."

"I'm a loyal friend and family member. There's a difference."

Just then, Enrique Alémán and his nephew Sergio came walking in the door with four Costilla Cartel militants who were dressed just like them in black Gucci business suits and dark sunglasses.

The smirk on Enrique's face and the bounce in his step told Pedro that there was good news.

"He's ours, Pedro. Finally. He doesn't have a clue that he's being watched." Enrique lit up a cigar and went to the mini bar to fix himself a drink. "I just got a text from Alexus. She's figuring out a way to tell Blake that she's coming back to Mexico to catch up with Gamuza and finish the job. Said she'll be here by morning."

Instinctively, Pedro took another gulp of champagne. He didn't need Alexus here. He was perfectly capable of running the Costilla Cartel by himself.

"Personally," Enrique continued, "I can't wait to see the look on Gamuza's pitiful old face when he realizes that it's over. He's been having our men murdered and beheaded for years. Now, it's his turn to face the music. Papi and Vida are smiling in their graves right now, I bet. I know they are."

"Why'd you bring Alexus into it?" Pedro asked. He got up, grabbing his white robe, and put it on as he stepped out of the Jacuzzi. "It was none of her business."

"What do you mean it's none of her business? She's still the queen, you know. Always will be." Enrique had his back to Pedro. He poured himself a shot of vodka and tossed it back. "It's destiny. Alexus was meant to be here to see this through. Just think of how hard Vida and Papi searched all through Mexico for Gamuza. It seemed like all hope was lost until this very day, and the two people who wanted him most are dead. Isn't that something?"

Pedro squinted thoughtfully at Enrique and turned up the gold bottle again. Seconds later Mary was behind him with her arms wrapped around the waist of his robe.

"Yeah," Pedro said. "It's something." He glanced at Sergio and the other four men.

Sergio was dumping a bag of peanut M&M's in his mouth.

Enrique sat down on a bar stool and spun around to look at Pedro, tossing back a second shot.

"I live for days like this, Pedro," he said. "Look at all we've managed to accomplish since Vida's death. The cartel is growing like never before. We've got new territory in all directions. We're the first cartel that's ever made the others join forces under the same umbrella." He laughed. "Even though that's not working out too well with the Zetas."

"I'll deal with the Zetas."

"I know you will, Pedro. I've got faith in you. Alexus does, too, believe it or not. You've always been the most loyal member of the Costilla family. Your loyalty is the glue that's held it all together for the past year or so."

"It really is," Sergio said, still chewing. "If the others had been as loyal to the family as you are they'd all still be alive today."

Enrique nodded his head in agreement. "Alexus was right to make you the boss. I knew she wouldn't let her sister in."

"She tried to," Pedro said.

Enrique and Sergio paused to look at Pedro, who was quickly growing tired of the chitchat.

"I made Mercedes give up her spot," Pedro said. "I'll shoot her right in the face if she ever so much as thinks she can take over the family business. I'm more than capable of running this operation. There was really no need to call in Alexus for Gamuza. It's my job to handle him now. Alexus retired, remember? She gave it all up to spend the rest of her life with that asshole husband of hers. You shouldn't have called her, Enrique. Next time ask me before you make any calls to Alexus. I really don't appreciate you going behind my back and calling her for something I could have easily handled."

"I didn't go behind your back," Enrique argued, standing up from the barstool. "I told you right in your face that I was calling her. I'll always call her. She's still the boss, no matter who she puts in charge. When Vida had Papi in charge, Vida was still the boss. You know how it goes. Nothing's changed."

"Something has changed." Pedro gave Mary the half-empty champagne bottle and sent her away. He waited until she was in the bedroom before turning back to Enrique. "You wanna know what's changed?"

"Tell me," Enrique said.

"What's changed is the fact that there's a real Mexican in charge again. Not some little girl from Texas. Not some fucking rap star from Chicago, or wherever the hell Blake's from. I'm the boss now, and I'll be damned if that ever changes. You understand that?"

Sergio's eyebrows came together.

Enrique squinted. "Alexus is the boss, Pedro. Don't let this little bit of power get to your head. You're doing great. Just keep running things the way you are now and everything will be just fine. Don't start feeling like you're God all of a sudden. Alexus can come back just as abruptly as she left."

The scowl on Pedro's face put the men standing before him on edge. One of Enrique's men flipped open his suit jacket to make his gun easily reachable in case there was a problem.

"I'd very much appreciate it if you all left my room," Pedro said, fighting the urge to pull his Desert Eagle and play target practice with his fellow cartel men.

"Whatever you say." Enrique raised his hands in surrender, let out a chuckle, and walked to the door. "Just do me a favor, will you? Tell Alexus what you did just now when she gets here. Tell her what you said. If you've got the guts."

Pedro stood there for a long while after Enrique and the others left, his teeth clenched tightly together, his hands balled into tight fists.

He glowered so hard at the door that he hardly noticed Mary had returned to his side until she was right up on him.

"Don't let them get to you, Pedro," she said in the softest tone of voice as she slipped a hand in his robe and rubbed his chest. "Do what I told you to do. Have something done to her. Then you'll be the boss of all bosses."

Chapter 14

Alexus's mother, Rita Mae Bishop, and the family shrink, Melonie Farr, were sitting in the family room drinking cocktails with attorney Britney Bostic when Blake and Alexus made it back home with the kids at 4:30 in the afternoon.

King and Vari took off running to their bedrooms to put away the many souvenirs they'd gotten from Jungle Island.

Alexus walked into the family room beside Blake wearing the widest smile she'd worn in forever. The quality time spent with Blake and the kids had her feeling like a real wife.

"Somebody's glowiiiiiing," Britney said as she got up and hugged Alexus. "I absolutely love it when you look this happy."

"So do I," Rita said.

"I'm just happy, that's all. With all the crap I've been through over the years, it feels good to just spend some time with my man and our little ones. He might get on my nerves" —she turned and regarded Blake with a brief scowl— "but I wouldn't change it for the world."

Blake hugged the girls and muttered something about the studio, then he left the girls to themselves.

"He never stays to talk with us anymore," Britney said. She poured Alexus a drink. "With his antisocial self."

"He's a creep." Alexus sat down, admiring the women's lovely white dresses. They were beginning to take after her with the all-white obsession. "We went to Jungle Island. The kids had fun."

"Doesn't it feel great to be away from all the cartel drama?" Rita asked.

"Yes," Alexus said, and turned up her drink.

She didn't stop drinking until it was all gone.

"Oh, Lord," Rita said. "Something's up. What's going on? You only drink like that when you're going through something."

"If Blake's cheating again," Melonie said, "I'll beat him up for you."

"It's not that," Alexus said.

Everyone leaned forward in their seats, anxiously awaiting the news.

Alexus wasn't sure if she wanted to tell them about her decision to go back to Mexico to take care of Gamuza. They would be judgmental. Momma would be hurt. So would Britney. They had been so happy when she left the cartel to be a housewife to Blake. She didn't want to see the disappointment in their eyes when she told them the truth about what was going on in Mexico.

"Come on," Britney said, patting a hand on Alexus's knee. "Tell us. What is it?"

"It's nothing, really. Pour me one more drink." Alexus held out her glass to Britney.

Rita came over and sat next to Alexus. She rubbed her only daughter's back for a couple of seconds, then pulled her in for a hug.

"Okay, okay," Alexus said. "It's the guy who killed my granddad in Mexico. We have him. They want me to fly in and...well, you know. Finish him off."

Rita pulled away and gasped. "But...I thought you said you were done? Why would you go back? You know how evil those people are."

"He's the one who sent those guys after you and the kids when I was in the hospital," Alexus said, turning to Rita. "We're not safe as long as he's still breathing. Me killing him will be the ultimate blow to the Zetas. They'll fold. Gamuza's been their boss for too many years to count. Let me go back and win this war. It'll be all over after this, I promise."

"No. No." Shaking her head vehemently, Rita got up and stormed out of the room, and Melonie rushed out after her.

"You're making a terrible mistake, Alexus. I mean it." Britney stood up and put her hands on her hips. She smelled like an orange covered in perfume. "You really need to reconsider this. There's no reason for you to go getting yourself involved with that cartel again. You've got all the money in the world. For Christ's sake, pay someone to do your dirty work. Stop putting yourself in danger. Be a professional for once. You've got well over $72 billion in legitimate cash and close to $200 billion altogether. If there's anything you need to be doing it's helping people and saving lives, not running around killing drug cartel bosses for things they did before you were ever even born. Be a thinker, Alexus. You're better than this."

"I know what I'm doing." Alexus put her face in the palms of her hands and took a minute to think.

She knew that the ladies were right. There was no real need for her to do anything herself. She had thousands of soldiers for that. Plus, she knew that Enrique would do anything for her. She only wanted to go to Mexico and handle Gamuza herself because it's what her father would've done. Papi had always believed in bloodying his own hands to teach the other cartel members that he was just as murderous as they were, if not more.

"I'll think on it," Alexus said finally. She got up. "Let me go and talk to Blake about it. I haven't told him yet."

She walked out of the family room with her head down, which was a good thing, because she narrowly missed stepping on one of King's small toy cars.

Chapter 15

'I heard a nigga got money on me
    Well I got double on him
    Got a fifty drum in my Glock 9
    He gon' make me dump it on him
    Hit Young Meach on Facetime
    You know we plottin' on straight crimes
    And we ain't duckin' no drama, nigga
    On King Neal, on Fin
    Ask everybody who know me
    Blake been a goon, young OG
    No reggie smoke, straight OG
    And you know dat pole stay on me
    Sold nine pieces and whole keys
    I done broke jaws, knocked out teeth
    And ain't nan nigga done hoed me
    In the strip club I'm Kobe
    Versace Mansion, we own that
    Niggas want smoke, we on that
    When I slide on em in that Bugatti
    Ain't no time to ask where dat pole at
    No talkin'... catch em slippin and T-Walk em
    You can't even come ridin' through where we walkin'
    Broad day, my heat sparkin'
    If it's three opps bring three coffins
    Line em up in the street and chalk em
    I'm cool as Will and you weak as Carlton
    Every time I'm in the club it's gang signs
    I'm always gon' claim mine
    Vice Lord till the day I go
    Been murkin niggas wit this same 9...'

Blake was in the booth again, this time without his team of local music engineers. He'd call them in later, but for now he could record by himself, with only his double Styrofoam cups of Lean on ice and the blunt he'd rolled earlier for company.

He looked over to the door as Alexus walked in. She looked so amazing in her tight-fitting white dress and heels. Her green eyes were just as captivating as they always were, but now they seemed troubled.

He stepped away from the mic and exited the booth.

"You a'ight, baby?" he asked, blowing smoke toward the ceiling.

"There's something I have to tell you," Alexus said. "It's about that phone call I got when we were at Jungle Island. It was Enrique."

Blake handed her the blunt and put a hand on her ass. "What about Enrique? It's some more crazy shit in Mexico?"

"They've found Gamuza." She hit the blunt and coughed twice. "It's for sure this time."

"I thought you retired from that shit?"

"I know."

He waited for an explanation but she gave none. He took a sip of the ice-cold Lean, looking her square in the eyes.

"So," he asked, "you plan on goin' back down there to handle that shit?"

She nodded her head. "Just this one last time. I won't stay long. It's just that Papi was so serious about getting this guy that I can't let it slide. I have to do it. For the family."

"I understand. When you wanna go? I'm ready now."

"You don't have to come."

"I'm not lettin' you go by yourself."

"It's not your beef, Blake. Stay here. I'll probably be back in a few hours. Or go to Chicago with Meach and Biggs. Take care of that fucker Cup while I get rid of Gamuza. That way both of our enemies can die on the same day. I'm sure you can get somebody to kill him."

"Oh, and you can't do the same with Gamuza?"

"It's not that I can't," Alexus said. "It's that I don't want to. I wanna do it myself."

Blake put his cups down on the soundboard and picked up Alexus by her bountiful butt cheeks. She wrapped her legs around his waist, and he walked her over to where his ashtray was. She dropped the blunt in the ashtray and kissed him on the mouth.

"You been drinkin'?" Blake asked.

"A few shots," she said.

"Drunk ass."

"You know how wet this pussy gets when I'm tipsy."

"No, I don't. Show me."

She dropped her Chanel bag and fumbled with his belt as he lifted her dress. They kissed and sucked each other's lips. She dropped her feet to the ground and yanked his pants and boxers down to his ankles.

"You owe me for this Mexico stunt," he said, looking down at her. "You ain't supposed to be goin' back."

"I owe you?"

"Mm hmm."

"Here, I'll pay you now," she said, and sucked his dick into her mouth.

He continued to gaze at her as she sucked him. Soon his dick was fully erect and slamming in and out of her throat.

He picked up his Lean and drank as she slurped him deeply. The email he'd gotten from Barbie came to mind but he quickly dismissed the thought. He wasn't going to call her. That was his final decision and he was sticking to it.

A few minutes passed. He put the cups down and picked Alexus back up. He carried her to the wall where his three platinum album plaques hung and guided his hard dick right into her warm, wet pussy.

She gasped as he entered her.

He started pounding in and out, in and out, and she gasped at his every thrust. Her fingernails dug in his back. She bit down on her bottom lip, moaning loudly because the beat to the song he'd been recording was still playing loudly and they both knew that no one would be able to hear her passionate screams.

Burying his face in the crook of her neck, he fucked her relentlessly, squeezing her meaty buttocks and breathing rapidly.

"Ow...ow...ow...ow..." Alexus moaned incessantly, holding on to his shoulders and looking down at his dick as he impaled her again and again.

"You want that honeymoon dick?" Blake asked, because she loved the way he'd fucked her senseless on their honeymoon.

"Yeaaaah," she moaned.

He kept on cramming his twelve inches in her for several more minutes, trying his best to make this just a quickie and not one of their usual hour-long events.

He was successful.

Just seven minutes later, according to his icy Hublot, he shot a thick load of cum in her and kept stroking until the very last drops were out of him.

He fell to the floor with her, and they laughed together.

"Jesus...Christ," she said breathlessly.

"That wasn't Jesus." Blake slapped her on the ass. "It might've felt like a miracle, but it wasn't God's son."

"Oh, shut up." Alexus pressed her lips to his, then frowned as he wiped his mouth after the kiss.

"Don't be kissin' on me after you just sucked on my dick," he said.

"Why not? It's yours."

"So the fuck what? It's still a dick! Ol' dick-suckin' ass girl."

"I can't stand your black ass." Alexus gave him a sharp slap to the jaw, and he retaliated by giving her an even harder slap on her ass.

For a moment they just stared at each other, out of breath and a little tired from their day out with the kids.

Alexus broke the silence. "I'm really done with the cartel. It's just this one last thing and I swear I'm done."

"I don't want you to leave, but if you feel that deeply about it then do you. I'm not gon' try to hold you back. I understand. Shit, if a nigga had cut off my granddaddy's head I'd wanna do the same to his ass, too."

"Yeah. It's kind of personal. I'm doing it for Papi. And for Granny Costilla. She's wanted that fucker Gamuza dead forever and a day."

"You sure you can't just have Enrique do it?"

She shook her head. "It has to be me. Nobody else. I'm the boss. Even though I'm done, I'll always be the boss, and it's my job to handle Gamuza in the same way he handled my grandfather."

Blake stuck out his bottom lip and nodded. "I feel you. Well, go ahead. Like I said, I'll be here."

"You better be. Don't go fucking no other bitches while I'm gone either."

"I'm with you until I'm gone now, baby. I told you that and I meant that. Ain't nothin' them hoes can do for me. You my baby. My queen. Fuck I need another bitch for when I got you?"

"I ask myself that question every time I catch your nasty ass fucking one of those sluts," Alexus said as she got up. She took a packet of wet wipes out of her bag and rubbed one between her legs until the fabric was covered soggy with semen.

Blake used one of the wipes for himself and then pulled up his Versace boxers and Balmain jeans. He was high off the Lean and Kush. For some reason he had the inclination to discard the song he'd just recorded. He thought it wasn't good enough. Maybe he'd just keep it with the hundreds of other songs he'd recorded and didn't release.

The weed had him thinking.

He sat down in the black leather swivel chair at the soundboard, checking his two iPhones while Alexus got herself together. There were two missed calls from his brother, Terrence "Streets" King, and one from Meach.

"I'll be back by morning," Alexus said, fixing her hair in the reflection of the booth's glass window. "I'm heading out for the airport now. Call me."

"I'll be here." Blake dialed Meach's number.

"You better be here when I get back, Blake. I'm not chasing your ass down again. Next time I'm just gonna say fuck you and keep it moving. There are way too many good men out there that will treat me like the queen I am to be chasing behind your dog ass."

Grinning, Blake flipped her a middle finger and ogled her jiggling derrière as she left out.

Meach answered: "Yooo."

"Y'all bump into dude yet?" Blake asked.

"Hell nah. Shit, we out west, bruh. Fuckin' wit' a few of the Lords in K-Town. Everybody whippin' foreigns. Let Cup pull up if he want to. We got twenty choppas, and all them bitches got a hun'ed or better in the drums. Get his shit flipped fuckin' around out this way."

"Just be on point, bruh. I might fly out there tonight if Rita watch the kids for me. Fuck it, I might as well. Wifey gon' be somewhere in Mexico till the morning. I need to get out this muhfuckin house for a few minutes."

"We out here, bruh. Just hit my line."

"Yup. Solid." Blake hit end and stared at his phone for a couple of seconds.

Then he said fuck it and dialed the number from the email.

Chapter 16

"Thank you, sir. Have a nice day," Tasia was saying at the drive-thru window of Burger King when her smartphone began vibrating on her hip.

She closed the window and looked at the phone.

The area code made her gasp.

It was a 219 number, the same area code that Blake always had.

She glanced back and saw that Jim, her manager — a long-eared young white man with thick glasses and a pale, pimply face — was standing behind her, smiling brightly and bossing Ebanee around at the counter. Jim could never go more than an hour without sneaking a peek at Tasia's ass. He said it reminded him of the old J Lo, whatever the hell that meant.

Quickly, Tasia answered the call and said, "Hold on one second."

She put the smartphone back in its case on her hip and requested a restroom break from Jim.

"Hurry up," he said, and she speed-walked to the employee's restroom in back.

In the restroom, she slammed the door shut and put the phone to her ear.

Her heart drummed in her chest.

"Hello?" she said.

She heard his chuckle and immediately knew that it was Blake.

"How did you meet Eb?" he asked.

"It's a long story."

"You in some kind of witness protection program?"

"Don't play stupid with me, Blake. You know damned well what happened. It's that psychotic wife of yours. She put the Mexican Mafia on my trail. I'm scared to go outside now. My name's not even Tasia anymore. Because of her, my whole identity had to be changed. And it's all your fault."

"My fault? How is that? All I did was fuck you good and take care of you."

"Yeah, and get me on some crazy bitch's hit list," Tasia said, her face tightening up in disgust at the sprinkles of urine on the toilet seat. "You have no fucking idea the shit I'm going through now. I haven't worn a high heel in weeks. I'm living around a bunch of dead-broke college kids. There's a fat, stinky bitch that lives across the hall from me who loves nothing more than to plop her fat ass down on my couch every chance she gets. I have roaches, Blake. Roaches! And I'm working at a goddamn fast food joint for nine dollars an hour."

Blake laughed like he'd just heard the funniest joke of the decade. "Damn, what happened to all that tough shit you was talkin' when I first warned you about Alexus?"

"Fuck you, Blake. That shit changed when my sister got shot."

"Where you at?"

"In Florida."

"Me, too. Where?"

"Can't tell you that. I can meet you, though." Tasia studied herself in the mirror over the sink, thinking of how unbelievable it was for her to be on a restroom break at Burger King to talk on the phone with a billionaire.

"I'm about to fly to Chicago," Blake said. "Taking my private jet. I can stop in your city and pick you up. You can fly there with me. I gotta be back in the morning."

"You gon' give me some of that donkey dong?"

"Can't do that," he said. "I'm back with Alexus, and I promised to be faithful. But I'll look out for you. Get you situated somewhere nice. Alexus ain't after you no more. She said she ain't comin' after nobody else I fuck with, she just gon' leave me if I cheat again."

"What about Ebanee?" Tasia asked, feeling more and more excited by the second. "She's here with me. That girl needs a blessing."

"I got y'all. Just pack up and be ready at the airport. Tell me where to meet y'all."

Following a moment of deep contemplation, Tasia said, "We'll just meet you in Chicago. I'm about to quit this cheap ass job right damn now. Hopefully I'll be able to get Ebanee to come with me."

"Let her know I'll get her a house and a car out there. Y'all could've been called and told me what was up."

"Maybe I did. You changed your number, asshole."

"Damn, I did." Blake chuckled once. "Look, you can leave that witness protection bullshit. Alexus ain't on that no more, and the Mexican Mafia ain't after you. Ol' scary ass."

"Fuck you, Blake."

"See you in Chicago."

"I'm on my way," Tasia said.

Her heart was still racing when she hung up and looked at herself in the mirror. She had just spoken to Bulletface. If she walked out into the restaurant and told everyone that, she'd be considered a lying fool, but it was true.

She remembered the days when she and her sister Fantasia had hated Alexus and Blake's guts for not disclosing any information on the whereabouts of their missing sister Jantasia; now, though, Tasia just wanted to live happily ever after. She wanted to go back to her life in Atlanta, stripping at Club Onyx and coming home with bags full of cash every night. This hillbilly lifestyle she was living here in Tallahassee wasn't cutting it.

She untucked her uniform shirt, threw the hat in the trash, and walked out of the bathroom with a new attitude.

"Eb, let's go, bitch. Fuck this job," she said when she made it back behind the counter.

Ebanee looked at Tasia like she'd lost her mind, and so did the other employees. Jim's forehead wrinkled up, and he put a hand on his hip.

"I got twenty grand for you as soon as we get back to my apartment," Tasia explained to Ebanee. "And for the record, my name is Tasia "Baddie Barbie" Olsen, not Jasmine. Jim, fuck you and this bullshit ass job. You need to use a whole bag of Q-tips in them long, nasty ass ears you got. And stop lookin' at all the girls like they're pieces of meat, you retarded freak."

Mouths dropped open and eyes went wide. Customers fell out of their chairs in laughter. Ebanee didn't seem to know what to do, so Tasia grabbed her by the wrist and pulled her along behind her as she left out of the first door.

"Don't you...you'd better not return!" Jim shouted after them. "I'll have the police here waiting!"

"Fuck you and the police!" Tasia flipped a middle finger and kicked the second door open.

The warm breeze of the outside air was welcoming.

"Girl," Ebanee said, "if you just made me lose my job and you don't really have that money for me when we get back to Eagle's Point, me and you are going to—"

"I have a lot more than twenty thousand dollars, Ebanee. I just told you who I am. I'm Baddie Barbie, the girl who was dating Bulletface a few weeks ago. I just got off the phone with him. He told me to tell you he'll buy us new cars and get us in new houses if we meet him in Chicago today. Here" —she handed Ebanee her smartphone as they made it to the SUV— "Call him back if you don't believe me. But do it while we're on the way to pack up our shit and leave."

Ebanee was was overwhelmed with joy when she dialed the number Blake had called from and heard his voice. He verified what Tasia had just told her.

They went home and packed a couple of bags — All Tasia took was her cash and a few changes of clothes — and an hour later they were sitting side by side on a flight to Chicago.

Chapter 17

It was raining in Cancun when Alexus stepped off her Gulfstream 650 private jet in Cancun, Mexico.

Enrique was waiting beside a white four-door Bugatti with the rear door open. He seemed to pay more attention to her than he usually did as he watched her walk down the stairs.

Sergio grabbed the two Chanel suitcases she'd packed for the quick trip and put them in the trunk.

"You are a queen, you know that?" Enrique said, not even trying to hide his admiration of her curves. "You were blessed with astonishing looks and wealth because you were meant to be a queen. Like Nefertiti. Like the queen of England."

Alexus laughed off the compliment and slipped into the rear seat. Enrique got in beside her and shut the door.

He wouldn't stop staring at her, so she put all her attention on her smartphone and scrolled down her Twitter feed.

"That kiss you gave me," he said, "when you first got out of the hospital. I'll never forget that, Alexus. Ever."

Oh, Lord, she thought. She had given Enrique a passionate kiss at the Matamoros mansion after she'd been released from the hospital in Los Angeles. She'd only done it because Blake was cheating on her at the time, and also because Enrique was so good-looking.

As he was today.

She kept her eyes on the phone.

"Watch out for Pedro," Enrique said. "He's letting the power get to his head. I don't trust him."

"Pedro's the most trustworthy person we've got," Alexus said.

Out of the corner of her eye, she saw Enrique shrug his shoulders.

Sergio got in the driver's seat and pulled off.

"People change," Enrique said.

"Not Pedro."

"Everyone changes when they want to. When it's best for them. He's not happy about me calling you in to deal with Gamuza."

Breathing in through her nose, Alexus noticed that Enrique was wearing a different cologne than the one he normally wore.

Why am I noticing his cologne? she asked herself with clenched teeth.

"He'll be fine." She turned to Enrique, twirling a lock of her long silky black hair around a forefinger. "You're talking as if there's something I should be worried about."

"Maybe there is."

She let his warning sink in; then, "Where's Gamuza?"

"We'll be there in ten minutes. Sit back. Relax. Enjoy the ride."

Alexus inhaled through her nose and exhaled through her mouth. She looked out her window. The resort was only a mile and a half away from the airport. She'd seen it from the sky as her plane was coming in for landing. After recent renovations and add-ons it was now worth over $800 million, a luxury vacation resort where people from all over the world came to have a good time.

As they were passing the resort, Enrique said, "How's Blake been treating you lately? I haven't been hearing from you. Things must be good."

"For now we're good. But you know him. His little girlfriend Barbie's in witness protection somewhere."

"You shouldn't have gone after her in the first place. Go after the man who put a ring on your finger and promised to be with you till death. Your problem's with him, not with those women."

"He's not going to cheat again." Alexus didn't want to look at Enrique. He was already too close, smelling and looking like a male runway model, assaulting her with his tantalizing build and ear-pleasing voice.

"Have you cheated on him?" he asked.

Her eyes went wide at the question and she was glad that she was turned away from him. She kept right on gazing out the window.

"I think you should do it," he pressed. "Just to see if that's what's been holding you back. It very well could be the reason you're putting up with him. Sometimes all it takes is some good loving from someone else to wake you up to what's real and what's not, you know what I mean?"

He waited.

Alexus wasn't talking.

"Answer me," Enrique said. His tone was calm yet incredibly demanding.

"I...I don't know, Enrique. Stop it. You're throwing me off. We need to be thinking about Gamuza. What if he escapes again? Like he did in Juarez? I can't have my name coming up in any more killings. Next time the Feds get me can easily be my last day of freedom.

"There's nothing to worry about with Gamuza. Our guys went in and secured the place before you landed. He's as good as dead."

It turned out that Enrique was right.

Sergio halted the car outside the front gate of a home that was surrounded by a tall brick wall. Alexus counted seven black SUVs parked all around the wall. The gate was charred and seemed to have been blasted open. A few Costilla Cartel militants that Alexus recognized were standing at the gate holding assault rifles.

"I should have worn a bulletproof vest," she murmured as Enrique got out and walked around to open her door.

She took the goldplated Desert Eagle out of her Chanel bag, put on a white cotton ski-mask, and then followed Enrique and Sergio into the compound. She cringed at the sight of a casually dressed man with his brains blown out just inside the gate. A few feet away from him lay a woman and a small boy, both with several large bullet holes in their shirts.

"You guys didn't have to kill the kid," Alexus murmured, automatically thinking of King Neal.

"That's his wife and son," Enrique said. "The guy by the gate was Gamuza's cousin. I ordered our guys to shoot everyone but Gamuza himself."

"Yeah, but still..." Alexus walked in Enrique's shadow, tensely holding her heavy golden gun. Again her heart was drumming, only this time it was from an adrenaline rush. Her eyes flicked in every direction as they entered the home, passing five more dead bodies with large holes in their chests and faces. Now that she was here in Cancun she wished she hadn't advised Blake to stay home. It was always comforting to have him at her side. She knew that Blake wasn't afraid of anything in the world. As much as she tried to put on a face of bravery, it didn't take a facial recognition specialist to see that sometimes she became scared. It wasn't often, but it happened here and there. She couldn't help it.

All of the troubling feelings escaped her as soon as she got a glimpse of Gamuza's bloody old face.

He was sitting in an easy chair with fifteen guns aimed at him. Pedro was standing behind the chair with his hands on the old man's shoulders. There was a bullet wound in Gamuza's left hand, and Alexus assumed that he'd gotten it as he reached for the Uzi submachine gun that was now on the floor in front of his left foot. He had the wounded hand cradled against his multicolored button-up shirt.

His eyes were replete with fear.

"So," Alexus said, "this is how it ends? With you looking all pitiful and miserable with a hole in your hand?"

"Say what you may," Gamuza said in a Spanish whisper, "but let it be known that Segovia cried like an infant upon his death, and I shall not shed a tear."

"Don't be so sure about that," Alexus said.

She took a step toward the old guy. He was every bit of 95 years old. Maybe a little older, definitely not a year younger. The hair that remained on his wrinkled head was a silverish white. Age spots covered his skin like the dots on a Dalmatian.

Raising the .50-caliber, Alexus was just about to blast a hole in the elderly cartel boss's knee when Pedro leapt to the side of the chair, bending low to pick up a gold machete from next to it.

It was the machete that had belonged to Alexus's father, goldplated with white diamonds and red rubies on the handle.

"Whoa, whoa, whoa. Watch what you're doing with that thing," Pedro said, directing his smartphone at Gamuza to film the old man's murder.

BOOM!

The Cocaine Princess 10

The bullet blasted through Gamuza's right kneecap, and he lurched forward, groaning in pain as blood spilled down to the hardwood floor.

Pedro grabbed Gamuza's shoulder and pushed him back in the chair.

"Are those tears I see?" Alexus said, smiling. She reached out for the machete, and Pedro gave it to her. "Lay him on the floor. Let's get this over with."

Gamuza began saying a prayer in Spanish as Pedro forced him face down to the floor: "God, I kindly ask that you allow this whore to go through more pain than she's ever gone through in the coming days..."

"Whore?!" Alexus swung the machete at the back of his neck with all her might.

Gamuza's head went rolling across the floor and landed on its severed neck against the door of a small steel safe next to the television.

The safe door was open a crack. Gritting her teeth, Alexus went to the safe and swung it open, sending Gamuza's head rolling again.

Inside the safe were dozens of pictures of Blake, along with the floorplan to what looked like a huge mansion.

It only took Alexus a few seconds to realize that it was Blake's Highland Park mansion in Chicago.

Chapter 18

When Blake made it to Chicago he had Meach, Biggs, Will Scrill, and Mocha — his team of platinum-selling Money Bagz Management recording artists — and ten more guys from his old Dub Life crew meet him at his Highland Park mansion.

He was sitting on the hood of his snow-white 2016 Bugatti Veyron Grand Sport, posting on Twitter, uploading photos to Instagram, sipping Lean from his stacked Styrofoams, and smoking a blunt of loud when the gang arrived in a fleet of white Bentleys, Ferraris, and Lamborghinis.

He had two Louis Vuitton duffle bags at his feet. Each one contained $400,000 in cash and Glock handguns with 30-round extended clips and 50-round drum magazines.

The 9 millimeter Glock on his lap also had a 50-shot drum.

"Yoooooooo," Meach said as he hopped out of his new Lamborghini Aventador, dressed like Blake in all white with a neck and wrist full of diamonds and holding a Styrofoam cup. A bad Hispanic girl in a MBM shirt and tight designer jeans over red bottoms got out of the passenger seat holding Meach's Louis duffle.

Biggs and Will Scrill were in Ferraris. They got out clad the same way, and they too had stunning women with them.

"I got the chefs in there cookin' steaks for us," Blake said, doing the Dub Life handshake with Meach.

Meach said, "I called Cup a few times. Nigga ain't answer."

"Fuck that nigga. This my city and I ain't even from here. Shit, every city I visit is my city. I run this shit. Let a nigga try to slide on me." Blake put his hand on the pistol. "I'm blowin' all fifty out this muhfucka."

"We ain't got no worries." Meach laughed.

Blake had his driver, an old school named Remo he'd met in the LaPorte County Jail, carry his duffles as he led everyone into the mansion through the garage, which had hardwood floors and two full basketball courts that hadn't been used in a while.

They went straight to the indoor swimming pool. It was where they always chilled and talked and partied. There was a full bar under a 500-inch wide-screen TV that played rap and R&B videos 24/7. A long white leather sofa stretched across one wall. The lounge chairs on either side of the pool were also white leather.

A Waka Flocka video was playing on the television. Everyone went to the sofa and started rolling and lighting blunts. A few of the girls went to the bar and returned with glasses and bottles of Hennessy and Rosé.

Blake sat between Meach and Biggs.

"You'll never guess who we ran into on Chicago Avenue," Meach said as his lady friend snapped pictures of the gang with his iPhone.

"Who?" Blake asked.

"Mercedes. Her and Porsche got matchin' Maybachs now. She got a lil team with her, too. Some 4's off Lake and Lockwood. She put them lil niggas on. I heard she a UE now, runnin' her whole neighborhood."

"Yeah?" Blake didn't like Mercedes. He didn't trust her. She'd tried setting him up to get killed twice in the past. "Fuck was she on?"

"Shit. Gave me her number, said she wanted to be in one of my videos."

"Hell nah. She ain't gon' be in nothin' Money Bagz drop. Snake ass bitch."

Meach laughed. "Awready."

The four personal chefs in charge of preparing Blake's daily meals came in with delicious plates of steak and lobster and a bunch of mouth-watering side dishes for everyone.

Blake ate voraciously. The Kush had him hungrier than usual.

He was finishing off a second sirloin when his smartphone rang.

Barbie was calling.

"Yeah," he answered.

"We're here. Should we get a cab?"

"Yeah. I'm at my spot in Highland Park. Come on through, and hurry up. We tryna slide out asap."

"Slide out where?"

"I don't know. Somewhere."

"Alexus isn't there, is she?"

"Do you honestly think I'd have you come here if she was here?"

Barbie did not answer right away. When she did, she only got two words out before Blake cut her off.

"I'm sorry—"

"Look, I ain't tryna fuck y'all or nothin' like that. I'm just lookin' out 'cause I put you through all that shit. It's my fault, and I'm makin' up for it. That's it, that's all."

There was another pause from Barbie. Blake stood up and walked to the edge of the swimming pool. He looked at his reflection in the rippling blue water.

"So," Barbie asked, "it's really over between us, huh? We can't even get it in one last time?"

"Nuh uh." Blake took a breath. "I love my wife. That woman has given me the world. All this shit is only possible because of her. Gotta give her the respect she deserves. I'm sorry. I shouldn't have been with you in the first place."

He heard Barbie sigh through the phone. "Okay, okay," she said. "I suppose I understand. She is your wife."

"She is."

"We're about to get a cab now. Thanks for the help. We appreciate it."

"No problem." Blake hit end and kept staring at himself in the water until Mocha appeared at his side a couple of seconds later.

Her tone was urgent.

"One of your maids said there's a group of guys climbing over the wall," Mocha said, putting a hand on Blake's shoulder. "And they have guns."

Blake clenched his teeth tightly together and turned to the gang.

"All the guys, get your guns and let's go." He snatched the Glock out of his Louis Vuitton shoulder holster. "Shit just got real."

Chapter 19

The men were five members of the Los Zetas drug cartel, one of the most feared criminal organizations in history. Together they had murdered 1,722 men in the past, about half by beheading, and today they intended to add to the body count.

They were here to murder the husband of the Costilla Cartel's top boss, the woman they both detested and admired. She was the world's wealthiest woman and also the Zetas' biggest enemy. Her cartel had taken over the drug trade during the past decade. She'd masterminded deals for cheap cocaine from all the Colombian drug cartels. She'd become a legitimate multibillionaire in the United States with her television corporation. She'd married the #1 rap star in the world.

On top of it all, she'd pissed off Gamuza, who'd ordered the five men to stake out Blake "Bulletface" King's Chicago mansion in the first place.

They'd been here, parked down the street with a pair of binoculars, for going on two weeks now.

Finally, their target had come.

Climbing over the tall redbrick wall, Eduardo Silva, the leader of the group, hoped this would be an easy mission. He'd been in the same room with Gamuza for hours on end as the boss planned the rap star's demise.

Eduardo and the four others would be paid $10 million for the rapper's murder. They had assault rifles with sound suppressors and 50-round banana clips strapped to their shoulders, Teflon vests under their shirts, and ice cubes in their eyes.

A skillful team of professional killers.

"Be swift on your feet," Eduardo said. "We're here for Blake King, but every person we encounter is a dead man. No mistakes. No exceptions."

Eduardo and the other Zetas had spotted Blake arriving nearly an hour ago.

Now was the time to move on their target.

They dropped down onto a well-kept lawn and sprinted toward the garage...just as a bunch of gunfire began raining down on them from the the roof of the mansion.

Chapter 20

Before heading up to the rooftop Blake had stopped in a bank-like vault where the mansion's previous owner — legendary Bulls player Michael Jordan — had once stored his many basketball trophies.

After purchasing the place, Blake had filled the safe with millions of dollars in drug money and guns, everything from .38 Specials to Tommy Guns and AK-47s.

Blake and Meach had fully-automatic Tommy Guns, each holding 150 hollow-tipped .45-caliber rounds in the drum magazines, when they went up to the rooftop. Biggs toted an AR-15 like Will Scrill.

They ducked low along the ledge of the roof, twenty feet away from the rarely used helipad, until the five men were close enough to fire on.

Then they rose and squeezed their triggers.

The gunshots were thunderous.

Two of the gunmen were able to look up and open fire, but it was far too late. They were mowed down from above. Bullet after bullet cracked open their skulls and shredded their limbs within seconds.

Blake was the last to stop shooting. Perhaps it was because he was past tired of people coming for his life. He had no idea who'd sent the gunmen but he he had a sneaking suspicion that it was either Cup or one of the Mexican drug cartels his wife was at odds with.

He stared down at the bullet-riddled men for a long while, adrenaline racing through his veins.

"Bitch ass niggas," he said, his nostrils flaring, smoke curling up in the air from the barrel of his machine gun.

Ten minutes later Barbie's yellow taxi cab pulled into the driveway. By then Blake and the gang were standing in the garage, and Chicago police were swarming around the estate.

Officers questioned everyone and no one was charged. Blake and Alexus were both licensed gun owners, and the five gunmen had obviously been up to no good. The guns used were taken for evidence. Witness statements were taken. Hundreds of pictures were snapped of the dead bodies. Two news choppers circled the estate from high above, no doubt recording footage for yet another breaking news story of murder and carnage at the famous rapper's home.

Blake stepped out of the garage to phone Alexus, ignoring Barbie and Ebanee, who were leaning against his Bugatti with Mocha and the other ladies. Alexus had called him twice while he and the gang were on the roof.

As soon as Alexus picked up the Facetime call she said, "I already know what happened. It's breaking news on CNN. Several gunmen reported dead in shooting at rapper Bulletface's Chicago home."

"Damn," Blake said, studying his wife's pretty face. "News travels quick around this bitch."

"It's why I was calling you. I knew it was going to happen. I finally caught up with Gamuza. Apparently he's been planning to get you for some time now. We found a bunch of papers. He'd somehow managed to obtain the floorplans for the Highland Park mansion and a few more of our homes. He even had the list of scheduled cities for that tour you canceled a few months ago."

"He dead?"

"Off with his head." Alexus snickered. She was in the backseat of a moving car. Blake could see buildings zooming by through the back window, and he noticed a speck of blood on her chin.

"So," she asked, "what's the death toll this time?"

"Five. They hopped over the wall. We got em from the roof."

"Jesus, why didn't you just stay in Miami?"

"Came to kick it with the guys."

"Well, you should've stayed to kick it with the kids."

"Listen, baby. I gotta tell you somethin', and you gotta promise not to get mad."

Alexus squinted. "I'm not making any promises."

"Barbie contacted me earlier. I had her fly out here to meet up with me."

"You son of a bitch."

"It ain't even like that. I'm just setting her up in a new house, since it was my fault she went into that witness protection shit in the first place. I told her I can't fuck with her like that no more, and that I love my—"

"Fuck you," Alexus said in an icy tone.

She hung up without another word.

Blake tried calling back thrice and all three times he got her voicemail. Either she'd turned off her phone or put it on airplane mode.

Shaking his head and gritting his teeth, he turned and walked over to Ebanee and Barbie, both of whom looked overly nervous. Meach was with them.

"Bruh," Blake said to Meach. "Take them shopping for new clothes and everything. Look up some homes and cars for sale on the internet and get one of each for both of em. Just send me the bill."

"What kinda cars?" Meach asked

"I don't care. Bentleys, Porsches— whatever they want. Just get em situated and send me the bill." He checked his phone again. "I gotta stay the fuck away from all my exes before wifey kills me."

Chapter 21

Enrique missed having Alexus Costilla as his boss. Sure, she was a lovestruck young girl with a horrible temper, but that made her no different than other cartel bosses. Underneath that concrete attitude of hers was a heart that was just as beautiful as her body.

He was next to her in the backseat of the Bugatti Galibier as Sergio pulled up to the Costilla Resort & Hotel behind Pedro's blacked out SUVs. She wore a scowl that had come when she'd talked to Blake a few minutes prior and had yet to fade away.

As Enrique was escorting Alexus into the building, he sent a text to the Cancun police chief's private phone letting him know that the Costilla family was now gone from Gamuza's compound and that it was now safe for police to respond to the murder scene.

It had been the police chief who gave up Gamuza's whereabouts late last week.

On the elevator, Alexus made it perfectly clear that she did not want to talk to anyone. All she wanted was a bottle of Hennessy and any pills they could find.

It didn't bother Enrique that Alexus was being so standoffish. He was glad just to see her here in Mexico where she was considered the queen by all who knew of her.

As soon as they made it to the presidential suite, she locked herself in the bathroom and didn't open the door until Enrique brought her the bottle of cognac and a Xanax pill Pedro had gotten from his girlfriend.

Alexus snatched the pill and the bottle and then slammed the door shut in Enrique's face.

"You alright in there?" Enrique asked. When Alexus didn't answer he continued. "You know something? We really miss you. Well, at least I do. I almost shed a tear the other night thinking about you. Pedro's such an asshole. He's letting the power get to his head. A few days ago he killed one of our best men, all because the guy failed to catch Mary when she slipped and fell. Dumb stuff, you know? I know, I'm not supposed to speak against the family, but you really should reconsider coming back. If you don't, I'm leaving."

He put a forearm on the door and rested his forehead on it. He wished Alexus would say something. Anything. He needed her more than she knew.

He smelled marijuana smoke coming from inside the bathroom.

"You know," he said, "back when I first became your grandmother's personal bodyguard, I never knew she had such a beautiful granddaughter who'd eventually take over things. When I first saw you I told Papi how beautiful I thought you were and he asked me if I liked having a head." Enrique laughed at the distant memory. "If only he could see you now. I know he must be so proud of you. I know I am. And you're getting prettier and prettier as the days pass by. I'm surprised Blake hasn't smartened up yet. Hell, if I were him, I'd be doing—"

Suddenly, the door went flying open. It happened so quickly that Enrique stumbled forward two steps before he looked up and saw Alexus.

His eyes went wide when he realized that she was naked.

And in the next instant, she grabbed him by the collar of his shirt, snatched him into the bathroom, and kicked the door back closed.

"I want you," she said, and kissed him, with tongue.

Enrique didn't hesitate to add his tongue to the mix. He tasted the liquor in her mouth. The Hennessy bottle was half empty on the marble floor. A smoldering joint of weed was on the sink.

Shit, Enrique thought. She drank half a fifth of Hennessy in a matter of minutes!

His hands found the massive butt cheeks that he'd previously only dreamed and daydreamed of feeling. They were softer than he ever could have imagined.

His dick grew hard immediately. Alexus practically ripped off his shirt and pants.

"Are you sure you want to—" he started.

"Yes."

Enrique had no more questions.

He lifted her up on the sink and slid inside her.

The warm, tight wetness of her love tunnel made his mouth fall open. He wasn't as well endowed as he wanted to be. Seven inches was all he had, but it was thick and apparently more than enough for Alexus, for she too gasped as he began plunging in and out of her, sucking and kissing her breasts and lips and neck, inhaling the alluring scent of her expensive perfume. She clawed at his back and pulled him deeper.

"Mmmmmm...yesssssss," she moaned as her body suddenly went still.

Her fingernails dug in his back. He felt her vaginal muscles contracting, and then a bunch of her sex juices came gushing out over his erection.

He kept thrusting his hips forward, going in as far as he could every time. It took him a few more seconds to realize that she was experiencing an orgasm. He'd seen "squirters" in porn movies but had never believed it to be true until now.

He pulled out and took a step back, staring in awe at her dripping pussy. Then he went to his knees and applied his tongue to her clitoris. She put her hands on his head and smashed his face against her juicy nookie.

"Hand me the bottle," she said, and he did as he was told and watched her take two big gulps of the strong liquor while he continued to lick her.

Her face became stringent. She gagged on the alcohol, and for a second Enrique thought she might vomit. Then she put the bottle down and gazed wantonly at him, biting her lower lip and palming the back of his head.

"That's right," she said. "Eat it. Eat this pussy. I know that's what you've been wanting to do anyway."

She was right. He'd been wanting to eat her pussy ever since she turned eighteen, maybe even a couple of months earlier than that.

He'd also wanted to dig his tongue into her asshole.

He did it without warning, and he saw the shock register on her face, but she didn't stop him. He tongued her there while rapidly rubbing his fingertips across her clitoris. He put a finger in her asshole, then two, then he stood and prodded the crown of his erection into the tight hole and smiled as she gasped and yelped.

"Go easy on me," she said. "I haven't done this before."

"You'll be fine. Just relax." He rubbed her abdomen and breasts, admiring her beauty as he slowly began to pump his dick into her asshole.

He'd hardly gotten in a minute of the anal exercise when his scrotum lifted and tightened. He went right on pumping as his semen spewed into her.

He grunted.

Alexus squirted again, and this time it splashed on his stomach.

He waited for his dick to stop twitching and spurting before stepping back.

His seed, thick and white and bubbly, spilled out of her asshole and splattered down onto the floor.

Chapter 22

'That gun on me, my nigga
       I keep it on me, my conjoined twin
       Ain't no more game playin'
       I'm a big dog, we grown men
       Opposition tried to slide on me
       Got shot down from the rooftop
       It's my ambitions as a rider
       All eyes on me, startin' to think I'm Tupac
       Bulletface, yeah dey call me dat 'cause some fuck niggas tried
to whack me
       Now they all dead, I got tall bread
       And I'm clappin' I ain't wit the actin'
       Like U-Haul I'm packin'
       Never one to lack, no I'm never lackin'
       Choppa yell "Cut!", pistol shout "Action!"
       Read a nigga well, don't need caption...'

"What you need is some damn help," Mocha said as she walked into the living room of her high-rise condo.

Blake had accompanied her to the condominium after they left the Highland Park mansion. Now, sitting on her hot pink leather sofa with his Styrofoams in hand, he was recording a new song on one of his iPhones, putting his frustrations into his music instead of lashing out the way he used to do.

Mocha's little white poodle was sitting at his feet, staring up at him as he rapped. The dog had been following him around since he first walked in the door.

"You all just killed five people," Mocha went on, "and here you are rapping about it already. Are you insane? Are you completely emotionless?"

Blake turned to look at Mocha. She was barefoot in a pair of blue jeans and a T-shirt. Her skin was dark brown and attractive. Her left nostril was pierced. Her shoulder was resting against the doorframe, and her arms were crossed over her chest.

113

"Why would I give a fuck about some niggas who came to kill me?" Blake asked.

"Who were those guys? Who sent them? The cop said they were all Mexicans."

"You just answered your own question."

"It doesn't make sense. You're the CEO of the biggest record label in the game right now. We're making millions every week. You really don't need to be getting involved with those kinds of people. We're a legitimate music empire. I'd like to keep it that way."

"There wouldn't be a Money Bagz Management without dirty money. I started this shit with half a billion in dirty money. You know that."

"It doesn't mean we have to be dirty with it," Mocha argued.

Blake waved her off and tried dialing Alexus's number again. He'd called her seven times since she hung up on him.

She still wasn't answering.

Mocha came over and sat Indian-style beside him. She picked up the television remote and started flipping through channels on her flat screen TV.

"I just don't understand it," she said. "All this nonsense. All these killings. It's not worth it. I signed with MBM to get some money. Not to get killed or shot over some shit I have absolutely nothing to do with."

"You signed to MBM and became the number-one R&B singer in the game. You signed with MBM to make some money and I made you a fuckin' millionaire. A multimillionaire." Blake turned his attention back to his phone. He wasn't going to debate over money with Mocha. She'd been flat broke when he signed her to MBM; now she was rich and famous, appearing on the covers of numerous Hip Hop magazine's as well as in videos along with some of the biggest names in music. Blake didn't like that Mocha rarely acknowledged the role he'd played in her success. "You know what it is, just like you knew what it was. Ain't shit changed but the numbers in your bank account. Don't sit here and act like I'm not the reason you're rich now. My plans, my shows did that shit." He shook his head. "Ungrateful," he muttered.

Mocha's attitude grew stronger; she sucked her teeth, and turned off the television. Blake felt her glowering eyes on the side of his face, as fiery as the two bullets that had gone in through his left cheek and exited the right one five years ago.

"I'm ungrateful? Really? I came to you because of my talent; not because I wanted your money, but to make my own bread using the voice God gave me! I don't see a lot of God in you or around you. All that murder is the devil, I don't care how much money I make. I'm not about to be ignorant and stay around this kind of mess. I want out."

Blake turned to her, brows furrowed, eyes incredulous. "What's that supposed to mean?"

"It means exactly what it sounds like. I'm done with MBM. I'm going independent. Already talked it out—"

"You still owe me three albums," Blake said quickly, suddenly remembering the contract.

"I want out, Blake. You can sue me or whatever. I don't care. I love myself too much to go through all this drama. You, Alexus, MBM— I don't want any parts of either of you."

"Gotta honor the contract," Blake said, cheerfully and with a blinging gold-and-diamond grin. He patted her on the thigh. "Look, you know I'm not dangerous or evil or any of that. It's the world we live in. It's the niggas comin' at me. The way the game is now, you need a nigga like me to keep everybody safe. Think of what would've happened if I didn't have all those straps at the mansion today. Think if we would've been unarmed when they came? Look at all the people gettin' killed all over the country. You can't even go out to see the movies no more without the fear of some weirdo goin' nuts and shootin' everybody. At least when I'm around you ain't gotta worry about your safety. You know the whole MBM gon' push wit' me. We'll always be tested, but I'm tellin' you...we are good. Let me handle this shit. Chill the fuck out."

Mocha cut the television back on and folded her arms across her chest again. She sucked her teeth and shook her head every time she passed a news channel with the breaking news of the Highland Park incident.

Seconds later the sound of a headboard crashing against the wall of the guest bedroom made them both chuckle and lightened the mood.

While the others had left for their own destinations, Will Scrill had followed them to the condo with his lady friend, and the two of them had gone straight to the guest bedroom.

"Bruh in there gettin' it," Blake said with a laugh.

"Nasty ass." Mocha shook her head. "He don't even know that girl."

"Stop hatin'."

"I'm not hating. It's the truth and you know it. He still got that girl in Gary thinkin' she's wifey and look at him, fucking every thot he runs across who got a fat ass and a cute face. Niggas fuckin' all these industry groupies are only further proof that niggas ain't shit."

"Bitches ain't shit, either." Blake always stuck to the bro code. "I'm sittin' here trippin' about Alexus not answerin' the phone and for all I know she could be laid up fuckin' somebody else."

"That girl ain't cheatin' on you. You really need to stop it."

"Remember I caught her cheatin' on me with T-Walk?"

Mocha had nothing to say to this. She'd seen the security camera video of Alexus sucking T-Walk's dick on the sofa in the living room of a home Alexus had in the city's Lawndale neighborhood.

"You got me there," Mocha said finally. "Damn. That was pretty fucked up. Especially since he was your biggest enemy."

"Who's to say she won't do it again?" Blake was checking out a news story on World Star Hip Hop about the Highland Park shooting.

"You're right." Mocha got up. "I have some pizza I made earlier. Want some? I'll warm it up."

Blake nodded and said that he did indeed want some pizza. "No pork, though," he added.

"I know, I know. It's beef," Mocha said as she disappeared into the kitchen.

Blake cast another glance at the dog. January Snow was his name. Mocha had introduced him at the door.

"The fuck you lookin' at?" Blake said, and stomped his fresh white Louboutin sneaker on the carpet to run the poodle away.

Instead January Snow took the stomp as an invitation to join Blake on the sofa. The first leap failed but the second one put him right next to Blake's two stacked up duffle bags. Then he made another leap onto the top duffle and lay down on his stomach, regarding Blake as if he were staring at a possible intruder.

"I don't trust your dog, Mocha," Blake shouted.

"He likes you," Mocha shouted back.

Blake chuckled.

Just then, his phone rang with a Facetime call from Meach, and he immediately paused, fearing that the call would be to tell him that the shopping trip with Barbie and Ebanee had been interrupted by a team of the Costilla Cartel's soldiers, sent on behalf of the queen herself to murder Blake's side chicks. Maybe they'd located the two women and did what Alexus had wanted to do to Bubbles.

One never knew with Alexus.

Blake answered and was relieved to see that Meach's camera was pointed at a black Bentley and a white Bentley that were idling back to back in traffic next to Meach's Lamborghini.

Barbie was in the white Bentley, and Ebanee was in the black one. Both girls now sported pricey sunglasses. They were waving and saying "Thank you, Blake!" at the camera until Meach turned it to his face.

"That's $560,000 you owe me for the whips and $81,422.81 for the clothes," Meach said, cheesing. "They say they wanna live together. Told em we'll do that shit tomorrow. But fuck that, you heard what just happened? With V-Walk and B-Walk?"

B-Walk and V-Walk were Brian and Victor Walkson, the brothers of Blake's old enemy Trintino Walkson who were currently in a northwest Indiana county jail with murder charges they got from an shootout with Blake and the gang. Biggs had been wounded in the shooting. Many others had been either killed or shot. Blake was initially charged with murder, but the charges were later dropped when it was found he acted out of self-defense, and that his weapon hadn't killed anyone.

"Nah, I ain't heard shit," Blake said.

"They just bonded out. Ten-million-dollar bond. You know T-Walk left all that money and dope to them. And then they robbed your wife's people for all them bricks. They got big bread like us, bruh. All the GD's talkin' 'bout ridin' wit' em."

"And?" Blake didn't care.

"I'm just lettin' you know, solid. They out here somewhere. That's just two more enemies we gotta watch out for, plus who-ever's with em."

"Nah," Blake said. "I ain't gotta watch out for nobody. They better watch out for me."

Chapter 23

The weather was incredibly sticky, almost too hot for Mercedes and Porsche's daily jog down Michigan Avenue, but Mercedes wasn't going to let anything get in the way of her exercise.

Porsche was getting better at it. At first she'd only been able to keep up for a short while before either pausing for a breath or shutting down completely. For the past week, she'd managed to stick it out to the end.

As usual, they showered and got their hair done in the customized half-million-dollar Mercedes Sprinter van after their run, but today they stayed on the Magnificent Mile for a shopping spree.

Gucci had quickly become one of Mercedes's favorite stores. She walked in with her phone to her ear, talking to two old friends on 3-way; they were on their way to Chicago to meet up with her and Porsche for a movie date.

She ended the call and said to Porsche, "It's a date."

"How I look?" Porsche spun around, swinging her slender hips. Like Mercedes, she donned a snug-fitting black Gucci dress over black heels by the same designer.

Although Mercedes hated to admit it, her little sister had grown more attractive and curvaceous over the past few months or so. Porsche's previously flat rump had some meat on it now, and her breasts were getting bigger. Her lips were fuller.

"Shut the hell up and shop, will you?" Mercedes said, beaming.

They went over to a row of bags. Mercedes glanced back to make sure that her guys were parked outside behind her Sprinter van and saw that they were.

She had two blacked out Escalades full of gun-toting young thugs who followed her around at all times.

Before she could turn back to the bags a college-aged white woman aimed an iPhone at her and flashed a picture. Four other shoppers were eyeing her closely. One of them whispered, "Isn't that Alexus?"

Mercedes gritted her teeth and said nothing. She and her paternal sister Alexus Costilla did look a lot alike, but she hated being mistaken for Alexus so often.

"So," Porsche asked, "what are we gon' do about the nigga Tremaine? He's still hounding us for dope like everybody don't know he the Feds."

"I know. I'll figure something out."

Tremaine was a high-ranking gang member from the south side, a Black P Stone who had long money but was also a rat. He'd been buying kilos of coke and heroin from Mercedes for a while now, and so far nothing had gone wrong, but he'd sent some other Stones to the federal penitentiary a few years ago and that didn't sit well with Mercedes.

She wanted him dead.

"I'll take care of him," she said.

"When?" Porsche asked. "When he got us both sitting in jail facing life?"

"I got this, okay?"

"If he comes to shop again I'll shoot the nigga my damn self."

Mercedes laughed.

She and Porsche visited three other stores before heading back to the van. By then she'd been asked if she was Alexus by seven more women.

"I had big dreams for that reality show," Porsche said as their driver pulled away from the curb.

"So did I...until Pedro came and threatened me, and sprayed our guys down on that corner. Forget about the reality show. We're already rich. Fuck being famous."

Porsche began scrolling through old photos in her smartphone's photo gallery, pictures of their deceased mother, and of Mercedes's deceased children. "One of these days I'm going to fuck that bitch Alexus up for all the pain she caused us."

"Fuck her, too," Mercedes said. She had tears in her eyes from looking at the pictures on Porsche's phone. "If all goes as planned today, that bitch will feel the same pain we've been feeling."

Chapter 24

Alexus and Enrique finished off the bottle of Hennessy together, then they had sex again, this time on the sofa and on the floor and finally ending on the edge of the Jacuzzi.

Afterward they cuddled up against each other on the sofa. The cognac had Alexus's head spinning so wildly that she fell asleep on Enrique's chest and didn't wake up until 8:07 PM.

Her belly was growling when she got up. Enrique was already woke and sitting at the computer desk in the corner. Alexus rushed off to the bathroom to clean up. She heard Enrique chuckle as she was digging her toothbrush and Colgate out of her Chanel bag.

"This shit isn't funny," she said.

"It is. It really is."

"Oh, shut up."

"May I ask how long you've been wanting to sleep with me? I'm curious." Enrique sounded amused.

"Seems to me like you're bicurious, all that poking around in my butthole. Freaky fucker. Order me something to eat."

She heard another chuckle.

She brushed her teeth and got in the shower. When she came out of the bathroom twenty minutes later room service was just leaving, and a seafood platter was waiting for her on the dining table.

"What's your girlfriend going to think about this little fling we just had?" Alexus asked as she sat down to eat.

"I'm guessing the same thing your husband will think if he ever finds out."

"I could really care less what Blake thinks. He's in Chicago with that Barbie bitch right now. I got a trick for his ass, though. He thinks I'm going to keep chasing behind him like some sad puppy, but I'm not doing it this time. I'm not going after his girlfriend, either. He can do what he wants, and I'll do what I want."

"I understand your frustration." Enrique got up from the computer desk and joined Alexus at the table. He sat across from her and watched her eat for a couple of minutes, then said, "What are we going to do now? Was that just a one time thing?"

Alexus shrugged.

"What's that supposed to mean?" Enrique asked.

Alexus didn't want to look up at him, so she kept her eyes on her food. "Let's not talk about this now, alright? There's a lot on my mind. I'm still pissed at Blake, and I'm not even sure if going back to our home in Miami is even an option. I might just fly the kids out here and move back in to the Matamoros mansion."

"That's the spirit!" Enrique pumped his hand triumphantly in the air. "Come back. Mexico needs you."

"Whatever. You just want me here to keep fucking me."

"That's not a bad idea, either."

Alexus rolled her eyes and ate lobster until she was stuffed. Then she scooted back in the chair and looked at Enrique.

He was far more handsome than she remembered him being before. His white shirt was unbuttoned and open. His face was clean shaven and perfectly proportioned with his lean body. She thought he looked a lot like soccer star David Beckham, just a tad bit darker and less muscular.

"Would you ever consider leaving Blake? For good, I mean." His tone was gentle yet demanding. He wanted answers.

"I seriously want to divorce him," Alexus said, with very little conviction.

"Then call Britney right now and tell her to start the process. She'll have it done by morning. You know she will. Leave him and come back home to the country you own."

"I don't own Mexico."

"Really?" He shook his head. "If you don't toughen up Pedro's going to run all over you. He's waiting on you to slip up. I'm telling you what I've been seeing. You need to come back and run this country with an iron fist, the way your grandmother did."

Alexus had to admit, Enrique had a point when it came to the divorce. Britney Bostic had one of the most well-known law firms in the world. Bostic & Staples was headquartered at the MTN Tower in downtown Chicago, and it had law offices in seven cities. Though Britney rarely stepped foot in the courtroom nowadays, she personally tended to all of Alexus and Rita's legal issues, as well as overseeing Costilla Corporation's many legal woes.

There was no doubt that Britney would have the divorce finalized in no time.

"I can't believe he actually brought that girl around him again," Alexus muttered. The more she thought about Barbie being in Chicago with Blake the angrier she became.

She took out her iPhone and called Britney. Enrique leaned forward in his chair, eager to hear her next words.

She did not let him down.

"I'd like to file for divorce as soon as possible. I'm serious this time. Get the paperwork started right this minute. I'll call you back."

Britney had no time to respond.

Alexus pressed end and dialed Rita's number. It rang thrice.

"Momma, Blake and I are done. I'm totally serious. He's in Chicago with that bitch again, and I'm not about to go at her. Not again. It's his fault, and I am done."

"Calm down, Alexus. And watch your mouth." Rita paused. "Who's he in Chicago with? I wish I'd have known that's what he was up to. I would've kept him here."

"You can't keep a man where he doesn't want to be."

"You're right." Another pause. "Hey, I'm on your side. If this is what you want then do it. But I'll tell you one thing, you are not going to leave these kids with me while you get this all figured out. And I don't want them staying in Mexico."

"Fine. I'll get a place in Brownsville."

"You might as well call that Mexico, too. Come on now, Lexi. You know Blake's going to keep Vari, and King does not need to be around those savages in Matamoros. I know that's where you'll be. If that's the case then I'll just keep King with me. Whatever I have to do to keep him out of harm's way I'll do it."

"You're making things seen worse than they truly are, Momma. My son is staying with me."

Rita sighed despondently. "Whatever you say. I suggest you think it over before you make any rash decisions. Talk to Melz and see what she thinks. You're acting off emotions. Call me back when you're not ready to kill Blake."

"Tell Melonie to fly here as soon as possible. Have her meet me at the resort in Cancun."

"How'd I know you were in Mexico?"

"Whatever, Momma. You sound like you're already siding with Blake. This isn't on me. I'm grown enough to make my own decisions. I know what's right and I know what's wrong."

"I'm not siding with anyone."

"Let me call you back, Momma."

"When you're calm?"

"Yeah. Love you."

Hanging up, Alexus doubted if any form of calm was in her future. The man she'd married had turned out to be a helpless cheater, and there was nothing she could do about it. She had to leave him.

She phoned Britney again, but only to tell the attorney that she'd be at the resort for the next few weeks or so.

Enrique's smile burgeoned when he heard the news.

"Don't get your hopes up." Alexus got up from the table. "Just because I'm thinking of moving back to Matamoros doesn't mean I'll be your sex slave."

"A sex slave isn't what I'm looking for. What I want is a queen."

Alexus didn't reply to Enrique's last words; the meaning of them was too powerful for her to ponder at the moment.

"Let's go," she said, putting the white ski-mask on the top of her head like a skullcap and grabbing her shoulder bag. Her iPhone began ringing. It was Blake calling again. She quickly ignored the call. Her eyes rose from the smartphone to Enrique, and she said, "Let's go and see if you're right about Pedro."

Chapter 25

Mercedes took her black Maybach Landaulet to the AMC River East movie theater. She and Porsche were in the backseat, smoking blunt after blunt in anticipation of their date.

"I wish Sasha wasn't so sick," Porsche said as she sent Sasha, her bisexual 17-year-old girlfriend, a text message.

Sasha had been sick with the flu for almost a week now.

"Girl, you ain't gon' think about Sasha when you see these niggas."

"Who are they? Do I know them?"

"You'll see." Mercedes put on a conspiratorial smile and told her driver, Shakema, to pull up next to a burnt orange Hummer that was parked near the theater's front entrance.

The Hummer H2 had huge 32-inch matching rims, and Mercedes wondered how her date was comfortable driving in such a flashy truck. Sure, her Maybach drew just as much attention, but at least it was classy. The H2 was a little too ratchet for her taste.

She understood, though. Her date and his brother were millionaire dope boys.

Porsche gasped as the two men got out of the Hummer and walked to her window. They were dressed in black and blue True Religion outfits with thick gold chains hanging from their necks. "T-Walk's brothers!" she said, shocked.

Mercedes nodded, smiling, and lowered the window. "Hey, how y'all doin'?" She gave them a wave.

"Ready to see this Ted 2," Victor said. He was the light-skinned Walkson brother. He and Brian shared the same father, but his mother was white and Brian's was a black woman.

Mercedes and Porsche got out and gave both men hugs. Victor walked next to Mercedes as they headed inside, and Porsche trailed behind them with B-Walk.

As they were purchasing snacks, a bunch of people started taking pictures of Mercedes and Porsche.

V-Walk laughed and said to Mercedes, "I bet you be feeling like Solange Knowles. This shit's wild."

"I hate that Alexus is my sister. I really can't even stand the bitch. Look at all this unnecessary ass attention she causes."

"Shit's wild."

"Yeah, it is. I'll be good, though." Mercedes selected a box of chocolate-covered raisins. "What was it you wanted to talk to me about?"

"I'll tell you once we're seated. You should already know what it is, though."

Mercedes hoped it had something to do with Blake or Alexus getting hurt. Not long ago, she'd set it up for the Walkson brothers to rob a shipment of the Costilla Cartel's drugs. They'd made off with thousands of kilos of pure Colombian cocaine.

Tonight she would be asking them to return the favor.

They found four empty seats in the fifth row from the front and sat down. Mercedes sat between Vic and Brian, and Porsche took to Brian's other side.

The previews were just starting.

"You know what I'm on," V-Walk said.

Mercedes nodded her head. "The same thing I want. Blake."

"That nigga gotta go."

"I agree. He's somewhere in Chicago. There was a shooting at his mansion today. Evidently we're not the only ones who want him dead."

"You can't find out where he at?"

"I might be able to, if Meach will tell me. I got his number earlier today. I can call him and see what he's up to. Nine times out of ten he's with Blake."

"You gotta do that. Them niggas killed my lil brother. I ain't letting that shit go."

"Good. I don't want you to let it go. I want that nigga dead just as bad as you do. He's the reason my baby daddy is dead, and that bitch Alexus had my mom killed."

"Damn." V-Walk tossed a handful of popcorn in his mouth. "It's all good. Hit that nigga Meach up and see if you can get that info."

"I'll text him when we leave," Mercedes said. "I can hit up Cup, too. I know he's looking all over for Blake." She giggled. "I had my guys shoot up his clubs while shouting out 'MBM Gang'. He thinks it was Blake's people."

V-Walk got a good laugh out of that. "I heard of Cup. My bro used to do business with him."

"Yeah, T-Walk was tight with him. He really runs most of Chicago. He actually got on from kidnapping Blake's daughter. Alexus paid a fifty-million-dollar ransom to get the little girl back. Cup's been on top ever since."

Mercedes was a big fan of the first Ted movie, so when Ted 2 started she got quiet and focused on the film, trying her best not to think about the wild sex she wanted to have with Victor. He was one of those pretty-boy hustlers, and she had a feeling that his sex game was off the chain.

Every couple of minutes or so she caught him staring at her thighs. She'd purposely picked the shortest dress in her closet for the date, and she wasn't wearing panties.

Thirty minutes into movie she glanced over at Brian and gasped in shock.

Porsche's head was bobbing up and down in B-Walk's lap. Her lips were sealed tight around his dick.

I know this trifling bitch ain't sucking this nigga's dick already, Mercedes thought as she looked at V-Walk to see if he'd peeped what was going on.

He was watching the movie.

She nudged him with her elbow, then slapped Porsche upside the head.

"Stop! Nasty ass."

Porsche raised her head and laughed, stroking B-Walk's thick erection in her hand until he put it away.

"Damn," Vic said, "can I get that kinda treatment?"

"Hell to the no." Mercedes was so disgusted with her sister that she didn't give Porsche another look until they were in the theater parking lot an hour later.

She snatched Porsche aside as soon as they made it to the May-bach.

"Respect yourself, big dummy. The hell is wrong with you?" Mercedes chastised, grabbing her hips in a fiery show of attitude.

Porsche only laughed, but her embarrassment was palpable; she couldn't even look Mercedes in the eye.

V-Walk came over and urged Mercedes to make the calls to Meach and Cup.

Reluctantly, Mercedes shifted her attention from Porsche to her iPhone and dialed Cup's number. She was still so upset with Porsche that she almost forgot what to say to him when he answered.

"What up, lil sis."

"You heard what went down at Blake's mansion?" Mercedes said.

"Yeah, I heard. Fuck that nigga. I'm tryna catch up with him, too. He ain't gon' live through what I got for him."

Mercedes's frown flipped over to a smirk. "Have any idea where he's at?" she asked.

"Nah, but Meach just called tryna keep the peace. I played it cool, told him about the reopening tonight at The Visionary Lounge. He say he might slide through. If he bring that nigga Blake wit' him it's closed casket, and if he don't it's closed casket for him. Either way it go I'm on that. Can't none of them niggas come to my club after they had it shot up in the first place. Especially to the reopening. That's like spittin' in my face."

"It really is." Mercedes high-fived V-Walk to let him know she'd struck gold. "You didn't tell me about no party. I wanna come."

"You can slide through. Bring yo' lil sister, too, that's my lil nigga. It's already startin'. Just pull up, y'all VIP."

"I'm on my way." Mercedes rushed into the backseat of her Maybach and told the Walkson brothers to follow her.

She rolled her eyes when Porsche decided to ride with them in the Hummer.

Chapter 26

The sun was going down when Meach, Biggs, and their girls made it to Mocha's place with Barbie and Ebanee.

Blake had begun to like January Snow by then, mostly because Mocha was watching The Notebook on Netflix and Blake thought the movie was too lame to enjoy. He was rubbing the dog's head and smoking a blunt, upset that Alexus still wasn't answering the phone.

Meach and the girls came in with four bottles of Patrón and Styrofoam trays from Harold's.

"Nuh uh," Blake said, shaking his head as Barbie and Ebanee walked toward him. "Y'all are not about to get fucked up and try to get me."

"Get you?" Barbie showed a knowing smile. "Nobody's out to get you. We just wanna have a good time, and thank you for the cars."

"Thank me from over there." He pointed to the kitchen.

Barbie and Ebanee cracked up laughing. They sat down on the sofa and immediately began filling cups with the liquor.

Meach said, "Cup havin' a party at The Visionary Lounge tonight. I think it's to celebrate the reopening. Wanna slide through and holla at him?"

"Hell muhfuckin yeah," Blake said. "See if he gon' say all that tough shit to my face."

"I got Mercedes's phone number now. We should catch up with her, too. I wanna crash Porsche's lil sexy ass."

"Bruh, didn't I tell you not to trust that bitch?" Blake gave Meach a serious stare. He sipped some Lean from his Styrofoam cups and blew out a stream of Kush smoke. "She ain't to be trusted, bruh. You know she set me up in Miami. Shit, she sent the same niggas at me who shot you and killed Young D!"

Meach's excited expression became dull. He reached for Blake's blunt, but Blake yanked it back and took another hit.

"Hell muhfuckin naw," Blake said. "You ain't hittin' my loud for that. You fuckin' with the enemy."

Meach didn't argue. He pulled out his own bag of Kush and a box of blunts and gave it to his girl to roll up.

Blake turned to Barbie. He unzipped one of his duffles (pushing the dog to the floor in the process) and started taking out ten-thousand-dollar packets of hundreds.

"How did you and her meet up?" he asked Barbie.

"She lived across the hall from me in that dirty-ass building the FBI put me in. They gave me a new identity and everything."

Ebanee said, "I thought her name was Jasmine."

Barbie shrugged, looking at Blake with an obvious lust in her eyes. "It's the name they gave me. I'm not even supposed to be around you. I was told that it was best for me to never contact you again."

"Why? I didn't come after you."

"Yeah, but Alexus did. I didn't tell on her but the Feds pretty much knew what it was about. Alexus had just caught those charges for running that Mexican cartel, and as soon as she came out of that coma those guys came at me. Doesn't take a rocket scientist to figure that one out."

Blake handed her ten of the packets of bank-new hundreds and gave the same amount to Ebanee.

"Y'all should be good with that. $100,000 apiece. Don't blow through it. Invest in a business." He put the tip of an index finger on Barbie's temple and pushed her head to the side. "Don't know why I bought you another car, I know you still got that Bentley I bought you in Atlanta."

"Thank you, daddy." Barbie tried kissing him on the cheek but he leaned away from her.

"Don't know where that mouth been," he said. "Y'all hurry up and eat so we can go."

"We already ate," Barbie said, biting the center of her bottom lip. "Now all I'm hungry for is you."

Blake shook his head and jumped up from the sofa, grabbing the straps of his duffle bags in one hand. He was not about to fuck up the good thing he had going with Alexus for a woman he was already in trouble for seeing.

Mocha decided against coming with them to the club, but the other MBM members were eager for the potential drama. Meach and Scrill took their guns out of their duffles and got them ready to fire.

As bad as Blake wanted to stay and have fun with Barbie and Ebanee, he forced himself to remain faithful to his wife. Plus, he knew he had to go and deal with the Cup situation. Just a few weeks ago Cup had threatened to kill Blake the next time he came to Chicago.

The girls stayed, and the guys —Blake, Biggs, Meach, and Will Scrill — left with promises to return soon.

Blake and Meach opened their trunks and pulled out AK-47 assault rifles with 73-round ProMag drum magazines, then the four of them piled into Scrill's matte black Bentley Mulsanne and headed for the club.

Sitting in back with Meach, Blake turned off his smartphones and briefly considered taking off all his jewelry as well. The drum full of bullets was heavy on his lap. He began filling his pockets with packets of hundreds from one of his duffles.

"The fuck you puttin' all that bread in your pockets for?" Meach asked.

"So I can show these niggas who the real king is. So I can show em money ain't shit. If they back down I'ma ball on em and if they don't I'ma lay em down." Blake lifted his assault rifle and turned it over, examining it, admiring it. "Niggas out here must've forgot how I laid niggas down all over the Midwest. I'm the muhfuckin king. If they don't know they gon' learn today."

Biggs said, "I been knowin' Cup since I was a kid. Hope he don't make us do him bad out there."

"That's definitely what the fuck it's gon' be, too." Blake came to the conclusion that he would keep his diamonds on. If he happened to catch a head shot when bullets popped off, he wanted to leave in style.

He cradled the heavy assault rifle and stared out his darkly tinted window as Scrill accelerated toward the west side of Chicago.

Chapter 27

Felicia Saunders had come to Cup's office on the second floor of The Visionary Lounge to interview for the bartending position she wanted in his legendary nightclub.

She was perfect for the job, a dark-skinned cutie with more ass than most of the strippers who worked for Cup at Redbone's. Her miniskirt and tiny shirt had already left little to the imagination, but now she was nude in the swivel chair behind Cup's desk, her knees pushed up by her ears, her face twisted in ecstasy as he slammed his hard man muscle in and out of her wet pussy.

"You...got...the...job," he said, thrusting his hips forward with every word spoken.

The circumstances under which Felicia was hired made them both laugh in between moans and groans.

Cup had only been going for ten minutes or so when he pulled out and sprayed her in the mouth with a healthy dose of protein.

He stumbled back against the desk and gawked at the stunning young woman's amazing curves as she got dressed.

"You can, uh, start tomorrow night. Ten dollars an hour cool?"

She nodded, dug in her purse for a wet wipe, and used it to clean the ropes of cum off her neck and chin.

"Be here at 4:00 PM sharp," he said, putting on his expensive slacks. He slid Felicia $400 before slapping her on the ass and watching her leave his office.

Cup was the type of gangster who always put business first and never came outside without wearing a business suit. He had just gotten his suit back together and sat down at his computer when someone knocked on the office door.

"It's Nona."

Cup frowned.

Nona's brother was Biggs, one of Blake's recording artists. A few years ago Nona had worked as a waitress at a number of Cup's nightclubs, but she'd hardly been around since she had started dating Blake a while back. Cup knew that Blake had more than likely made sure Nona was set for life and didn't need a job.

"It's open. Come in." Cup leaned back in his chair as Nona walked in, wearing a black dress with a ninety-thousand-dollar Birkin bag under her arm. Cup knew the price because he'd bought the mother of his children the exact same bag not even a week prior.

"We need to talk before my brother gets here," she said. "You already know how much he respects you and your reputation. Y'all both are Vice Lords. You know he's signed to Blake's company, and Blake is also a Vice Lord. It doesn't make sense that you all are into it over nothing. Mercedes set this shit up to go down like this. I was there at Porsche's condo when Mercedes made the call to her guys and told them to shoot up your clubs. You're mad at the wrong person, Cup. Blake had nothing to do with it. It was all Mercedes."

"So," Cup said, easing back a little more in his chair as his expression became thoughtful, "it was Mercedes who set it all up?" He'd already thought it was strange that she had phoned him on the same night of the club shooting.

"Yeah, she was standing at the window talking while me and Bubbles were taking shots and tripping over those nutcases Alexus had sent after us, the guys who beheaded those two cops. I heard everything she said. As a matter of fact, we had just left Redbone's."

"Hmm." Cup nodded his head and opened the bottom drawer on the right side of his desk.

In the drawer was a fully-automatic Glock 33. It was a sub-compact .357 pistol with an extended 20-round magazine. He picked it up as he stood and tucked it in the back of his pants.

"You see all the celebrities in VIP?" he said as he walked Nona to the door.

"I don't care who's in VIP. Make sure nothing happens to my brother, Cup. That's all I care about. Don't put him in a position where he's forced to choose between you and Blake, because he's signed to MBM. It's what pays his bills, what made him a millionaire."

"Say no more. I got it all figured out now." Cup opened the door and stepped aside for Nona to lead the way.

Nona's eyes went wide as she exited the office.

Standing just outside the door were two Chicago police officers.

Chapter 28

Alexus pounded at the door of Pedro's suite with Enrique and five of the Costilla Cartel's men in black suits lingering behind her.

Mary, Pedro's girlfriend, opened the door wearing a robe and a bright smile. "He's gone. Went to the car dealership down the road to pick up the Maserati convertible he just bought me."

Alexus pushed the door open, hitting Mary in the face with it. Mary stumbled back and grabbed her aching face.

"What's been going on with my cousin?" Alexus barged into the suite with her goldplated Desert Eagle in hand, clenching her teeth together in a tight scowl. "He was loyal before. Have you been filling his head with bullshit? Because if you're talking against me and making him not like me for some reason I'm going to cut off your fucking head and feed it to your mother."

"I don't...I don't know what you're talking about. He loves you," Mary said, her voice cracking.

"Come on." Alexus pointed the gun at Mary's face. "You're coming with us to the dealership."

"Let me get dressed," Mary pleaded as tears sprouted forth from her eyes.

Alexus shook her head. "The robe is fine. Let's go. Right the fuck now."

The golden .50-caliber didn't get put away until they were on the elevator seconds later. Alexus tucked it in her Chanel bag and dialed Pedro's number. When he picked up she said, "Are you still at the dealership?"

"Yeah. Why? How'd you know that?"

"I asked Mary." Alexus grinned at the terrified girl. "Which dealership is it? We're on our way. I've been thinking of getting some new wheels."

"Alameda's Exotics. It's on Fernando Boulevard."

"On my way."

The elevator made it to the lobby, and the doors parted.

"Make a scene and you're dead," Alexus whispered in Mary's ear as they crossed the lobby.

Dozens of people recognized Alexus as she sauntered past them. They took pictures and shouted her name, but she ignored them like usual and kept walking until they were climbing in the four-door Bugatti.

Sergio was fast asleep in the driver's seat. Enrique got in next to him and shook him awake.

Alexus took the gun out again and pressed it to Mary's ribcage. "Don't you fucking move. I remember that little attitude you had with me a few weeks ago. I told you I'm the queen of the fucking world, didn't I? Just because you're sucking my cousin's dick doesn't make you family. You're a peasant to me. I'll murder you and won't think twice about it, you understand that?"

"Yes...yes I understand. I'm sorry for what I said. I was just...I wanted him to be the top guy. That's it. I wasn't thinking."

Alexus's brows came together; she had no idea what Mary was talking about.

"Tell me everything you said, Mary. And don't lie. I've had microphones put in every room Pedro has been in lately, so I'll know if you're lying."

The lie was spur of the moment. Alexus was fishing for information.

Sobbing hysterically, Mary spilled her guts. "I told him to get rid of you...so he could take over. I don't know what I was thinking. I think I was high and drunk. Please don't—"

Alexus balled the collar of Mary's robe in her fist and slapped her across the head with the gun.

Mary screamed as Sergio sped off down a side road. Blood dripped down the side of her face and ruined the clean white robe.

The corner of Alexus's mouth rose in an expression of disgust and anger. She grinded her teeth together. The revelation that Mary had practically told Pedro to kill her had Alexus fuming. She was tempted to blow Mary's brains right out the rear driver's side window, but she kept her cool and glanced back at the black SUV that was following them.

"Enrique," she asked, "are those men behind us under you or have they been with Pedro?"

"They're my best guys. Nothing to worry about."

"Good." Because Alexus would've had Sergio pull over so she could kill them otherwise.

She turned back to Mary and glowered at the frail young woman all the way to the dealership.

King Rio

Chapter 29

"Here you go. I want the Porsche 911 and the Maserati," Pedro said, taking in a big cloud of smoke from his Cuban cigar.

He slid his black American Express card across the table to the car saleswoman. She was an overweight Mexican woman with a pleasant smile and a chunky diamond ring.

"That'll be $442,954.56," she said in her tiny voice.

Pedro nodded and turned to take another look at the dark red Porsche he was buying for himself. It was in the middle of the showroom floor, its flawless paint gleaming.

He thought of how he'd look speeding through Mexico with Mary at his side. Although he wasn't the ultimate boss of The Costilla Cartel, he was the head man in charge. All orders were made by him. All deals were made by him. At the end of the day he was the boss, and that fact alone brought a glow to his brown visage. He turned and gazed outside at his men. It occurred to him that maybe he'd be able to convince one or two of them to join him in his plot to murder Alexus, but then he shook his head no. The Costilla Cartel's soldiers were trained to obey the top boss above anyone else. If he ordered them to kill Alexus, or even to simply help him do it, they would more than likely turn their guns on him, and he'd be the dead man.

"Here's your receipt, sir. And the keys," the portly car saleswoman said.

Pedro took the receipt and the keys and tossed the key to the Maserati to one of the three men who'd accompanied him into the dealership.

Just then, he saw the white Bugatti Galibier that Alexus had arrived to Gamuza's place in. It was pulling into the parking lot ahead of a black Tahoe, one of the vehicles he himself had purchased for his security.

Instead of getting in the Porsche as he'd intended, he walked out the door with his arms outstretched for a hug from his little cousin as she got out of the Bugatti.

Then he saw Mary's tear-streaked face in the backseat, and his hands dropped.

"You're a dirty son of a bitch, Pedro. You know that?" Alexus hissed.

Pedro's breathing stopped when Alexus tugged her Desert Eagle out of her purse. He wondered what had happened.

"What did I—" he started.

"You sneaky fucker, you know exactly what the fuck you did. Enrique! Drag that bitch out of the car!"

Pedro had no choice but to watch helplessly as Enrique got out of the passenger seat, went to Mary's door, snatched it open, and dragged her out by her hair. He threw her on the ground in front of Alexus.

"You plotting on me?" Alexus's nostrils flared. "Do you think you can take over some shit? In MY country?!"

The car dealership's employees began lining up at the glass windows. The cartel militants who came with him drew their guns and hesitated before taking aim at him.

Then Alexus did the unthinkable.

She pointed the gun at Mary and pulled the trigger.

The gunshot was so loud that it stunned Pedro.

Mary's brains went sliding across the rain-slick gravel.

"Keep fucking with me and you'll get the exact same treatment," Alexus said before she climbed back in the Bugatti.

Pedro could not help but to cry as Sergio sped away. Most of his men abandoned him and followed Alexus in their SUVs.

He was left staring emptily at Mary's exploded head. He blamed himself for her death, and he vowed to one day get even with Alexus for killing the only woman he'd ever loved.

Chapter 30

'...Baby girl these diamonds are not phony
    This car I got came from Barcelona
    These shoes I got came from fuckin' Paris
    This bitch mad 'cause I don't do marriage
    Let a nigga slide, no we don't do scaries
    We tote pistols, no we don't do worries...'

With Sosa's "Faneto" blasting from the H2 Hummer's speakers, and B-Walk's dick in her pussy, Porsche was both turned up and turned on as she lay on her back in the backseat.

B-Walk was fucking her senseless. They'd only been at it for about ten minutes and already Porsche knew that his was the best dick she'd ever had, and she'd had quite a few.

She gazed out the open sunroof as he pounded her juice box. Her phone was ringing with a call from Mercedes, but she wasn't about to answer it. Sis knew what was going on. Porsche didn't consider herself a slut or thot or bustdown or whatever, but she couldn't deny the fact that she loved sex. It was the only thing that truly made her feel good, whether it was with a man or a woman. She'd taught her girlfriend Sasha more than enough about eating pussy, but it was still good to feel a man inside her.

"Hurry up, bruh," Victor said from the driver's seat, "we're almost there."

"I'm almost...done," B-Walk said as he pulled back and filled the condom he had on with a load of semen.

Porsche felt great. She'd orgasmed twice. She looked up at B-Walk, pinching her nipples and biting her bottom lip.

"Now," she said, "that's how you fuck a bitch. Especially on the first date. Make me wanna come back for more."

B-Walk laughed as he stroked the rest of his cum into the rubber and then snatched it off.

They got dressed. Porsche lit a cigarette and stared straight ahead as V-Walk drove down Chicago Avenue behind her sister's Maybach.

"Let me call this hoe back," she said, picking up her smartphone. "Her dumbass ain't even got us no security out here. If shit goes down we'll be fucked up."

As the phone was ringing at her ear, she watched V-Walk take a gun out of the glove compartment, and B-Walk pulled an assault rifle from behind the backseat.

Mercedes answered: "Nasty hoe. Answer the phone next time."

"I had it in my purse," Porsche lied. "Call the guys before we make it to this club. Ain't no telling what's gonna pop off."

"Bitch, I'm good. I got my strap. You got yours. Just be ready to pull it out if you need to."

"You think Blake gon' show up with Meach?"

"If he does it's over for him."

Porsche sighed. She didn't agree with Mercedes about their security situation, but she knew that Mercedes wasn't going to change her mind.

The Visionary Lounge was five blocks away. Cars were lined up all along the avenue. Dozens of people in their freshest outfits were walking toward the nightclub.

"I just heard on the radio that everybody's going to be performing at the club tonight," Mercedes said. "King Louie, Common, Dreezy, Chance the Rapper, Jeezy, Lil Wayne, and some more people. That's why it's so crowded out here."

"I don't care. I just wanna see Blake show up and get his fuckin' issue. Hope they whack his bitch ass."

B-Walk said, "Ain't no hoping to it. If we see that nigga he gone."

"We'll be in VIP," Mercedes said, "so we'll see everybody. Keep your ass next to me all night. I don't want us to get separated. Shit can go down at any minute."

"I'll be good," Porsche said. "Just pull over now and I'll get in with you."

"I'm not pulling over. Your trifling ass should've got in with me at the theater."

Mercedes hung up, and Porsche sucked her teeth and dropped the phone in her purse. She lifted out the 9 millimeter Glock hand-gun Mercedes had given her a few weeks ago and held it in the palm of her hand.

She muttered a prayer as they pulled up in front of the night-club, a prayer of safety for herself and Mercedes. Then she put the gun back in her purse and looked out her window.

The line of people waiting to get in stretched for two blocks.

There were two policemen in uniform walking back and forth near their squad car in the KFC parking lot across the street. A black, four-door Bentley with darkly tinted windows was cruising past, and Porsche guessed that it was probably one of the rappers arriving.

Cup was standing at the front door with Lil Cholly, one of his closest friends. Mercedes had dated Cholly for about a month back when they were still poor and living with their mother in the building on Lake and Lockwood. Then Cholly had fucked a girl who'd gone to school with Mercedes, and she broke up with him. Since then they had remained friends for the most part. He'd helped out with the rent and other bills on several occasions. Like Cup, Cholly was dapper in a spotless white business suit.

B-Walk said, "You can go ahead and get out. We'll be driving up and down the avenue, lookin' for that nigga Bulletface. Give me a call if you see him or one of them other niggas. Let me know what kinda car you see em in if you can, or if you see em in the club let me know so we can pull up and wait."

"I gotchoo," Porsche said. "Just make sure the nigga dies this time. He's been shot a bunch of times before and they haven't been able to kill his ass yet."

B-Walk chambered a round in the assault rifle. "This choppa gon' get him all the way through there. I can bet money on that."

A nervous laugh was Porsche's only reply.

Cup shouted for her as she climbed out of the Hummer and walked to the Maybach. She waved and gave him a smile. "Hey, Cup. Hey, Lil Cholly," she said.

"I see you gettin' thick," Cholly shouted back.

Mercedes stepped out of the Maybach looking like a million bucks. Unable to mask their excitement, many of the girls standing in line began waving and yelling at Mercedes. To them she represented success. She was one of the only people who'd made it out of the hood, certainly the only millionaire, and she hadn't changed. She came back and gave back, and that was enough to gain her even more respect than she had when she was flat broke.

They crossed the busy avenue and went right into the club with Cholly and Cup.

The place was so packed that Porsche wondered how all the folks lined up outside would fit.

"I've been waiting on you two to show up," Cup said, slipping an arm around Porsche's shoulders. "We got a whole lot of money in here tonight. Big money." He turned to Porsche. "Speaking of big money, word on the street is that you owe some big money to the BDs out in Englewood. They say you stole some dope from some guy you had been fucking and that it belonged to the gang. Be careful. Tadoe and a few more BDs are on their way here."

Porsche's eyes widened in horror. "Did they say Glo was coming?"

"As a matter of fact they did. Why, is he the guy?"

"Yeah. He busted my head, so I took everything and left."

"Was that the dope you sold me a few weeks ago?"

Porsche nodded sheepishly. They were making their way toward the upstairs VIP section. Lil Wayne was already onstage performing "Glory", a song off his upcoming Free Weezy Album.

"I'll take care of that," Cup said, patting Porsche on the back. "I need to talk with y'all in my office about some business, anyway. Come on up."

He led the way up the stairs. Mercedes paused on the third stair and waited until Porsche was next to her.

"Be ready," Mercedes whispered in Porsche's ear. "I don't know what's going on, so just be ready, alright?"

Porsche nodded and patted the side of her purse. "We're good, sis. Nothing to worry about."

But Mercedes was definitely worried. Porsche could see it in her big sister's eyes, the way she kept looking around as if someone was out to get her.

They went past the VIP's glass door. Porsche glanced in and caught a glimpse of Jeezy popping open a bottle of Ace.

Then they kept going and turned left into a short hallway that led to Cup's office.

It was the last thing Porsche remembered before the darkness.

Chapter 31

"We ain't gon' catch up with the nigga ridin' up and down the street like this, bruh. We don't even know what kinda car he's drivin'," B-Walk said.

"He got a Bugatti," V-Walk said. "Just keep your eyes out for a Bugatti. You know how he like to stunt. It'll be that Bugatti."

"Bruh, the man is a fuckin' billionaire. I'm pretty sure he got more than one car."

"Just shut the fuck up and look. Damn, nigga."

B-Walk shut the fuck up and looked around. They were passing a McDonald's restaurant on Chicago Avenue. A blue Rolls-Royce caught his attention, and he leaned out his window to get a closer look at the driver and passenger.

It was a rapper he'd once seen at a concert in Dallas, Texas. Chedda Da Connect, the Flicka Da Wrist guy, and Louisiana rapper Kevin Gates was in the passenger seat.

"Shit, that's Kevin Gates!" B-Walk said. "Man, we need to be in the club. It's crackin' in that muhfucka. I wonder who else gon' be up in there. Bet it's a gang o' bad bitches. Probably some hoes we been wantin' to fuck. Lauren London might be in there, for all we know."

"I'm turnin' around. Fuck it. You might be right. Shit, Blake might already be in the club."

"If he is I'm shootin' that nigga right in front of everybody. Fuck all the bullshit. Ain't no nigga gon' kill my lil brother and get away with it."

V-Walk nodded his head, his teeth clenched together, his eyes glued to the road. He agreed with Brian. There was nothing to really be afraid of. They were already facing murder charges in Indiana, charges that they would certainly be found guilty of when trial came. They were both willing to murder Blake on sight, no matter if the rap star was surrounded by cops or surrounded by fans. It didn't matter. All that mattered was that Blake "Bulletface" King died in the same way that Trintino "T-Walk" Walkson had died.

"Hope they don't recognize our truck," V-Walk said as he busted a U-turn and headed back toward the club.

He hardly noticed the black Bentley that drove up alongside his door, and when he did it was too late.

The drumming and flashes of fully-automatic gunfire told him that his life was over.

In the final second of his existence, he saw Blake's face behind the AK-47 that sent both him and his brother to their maker.

Chapter 32

Lil Cholly had faked like he was talking on his smartphone as he rounded the corner into the hallway behind Porsche.

Then he'd pulled the foot-long lead pipe from out of his pants and whacked her hard across the back of the head with it.

She went down instantly.

Mercedes only managed a half-turn before she too was knocked out by a blow from the pipe.

Cholly and Cup dragged the girls into the office where two policemen were waiting with their handcuffs ready. They were the officers who'd been waiting outside the office when Nona was leaving the office, cops who'd been on Cup's payroll for years.

Officer Dan Hubbard, a corpulent white man with thin-framed glasses and a heavy beard, was a twenty-year veteran of the CPD. His partner John Ivy was black and just as heavy but more muscular in the arms.

Cup handed them two envelopes, each containing $20,000 cash.

"I don't wanna see them again," Cup said as the policemen cuffed Mercedes and Porsche's hands behind their backs. "And no, I don't mean send them away. Kill them. Throw them in the woods somewhere. I don't care what you do, just make sure they don't live to see another day. Take those purses with you. Destroy all the evidence. Do that and I've got $80,000 more for each of you."

"Since there's sure to be someone who remembers seeing them enter the club," Officer Hubbard said, "we'll file the necessary paperwork and say we escorted them out of the club for being too intoxicated and disruptive, or something like that. Instead of arresting them we took them home, you know. It was the last time we saw them. Guess some guys beat them to death shortly afterwards."

Cup plopped down in his swivel chair and watched the officers drag the girls out of the office and down the stairs to the club's rear exit door.

"That was easy, wasn't it?" Cup said, blowing out a breath as Lil Cholly wrapped the pipe in a bath towel.

"I liked Mercedes," Lil Cholly said, shaking his head. "Damn. Fucked up how shit gotta go sometimes."

"Yeah, it is. She had my businesses riddled with bullets. A snake like her has no business around us. There's no telling what would've happened had Blake shown up with his goons."

"I know." Cholly sounded down. "Bitch should've minded her muhfuckin business, or got at that nigga herself. Didn't understand that we make millions with that nigga."

"Some people have to learn the hard way."

"We still have beef with Blake. This won't change a thing."

"Yeah, but it'll cut off the snake that started it. I'll talk to Blake. Get this shit squashed so we can get back to the money. We're almost out of dope."

Suddenly, the club became louder. People were chanting something.

Lil Cholly pointed at the row of camera monitors on the wall behind Cup's desk.

"Well," Lil Cholly said, "at least we won't have to go looking for him."

Cup spun around in his chair and looked at the monitors just as he realized what the people were chanting.

Chapter 33

"Bull-et-face! Bull-et-face! Bull-et-face!..."

It seemed like everyone in the club was shouting his name as he made his way through the crowd with Meach, Biggs, and Will Scrill leading the way.

Seconds later the Meek Mill track that was blasting throughout the nightclub was replaced by a Bulletface club banger.

Blake kept looking up to the VIP section to see if Cup was up there. Though he could not quite tell who was all there, he knew that Cup wasn't one of them.

The big boss Rick Ross was standing in the middle of the massive floor with Meek Mill and Nicki Minaj. Blake hugged Nicki and said a few words to Ross and Meek. He'd admired Ross's hustle for a long time and it was always a blessing to see the fat guy in person. Tonight he and Ross boasted the thickest diamond necklaces in the building, though the ten-carat white diamonds in Blake's were much more expensive.

He mingled with the fans and took more than a hundred pictures with them before ordering five hundred bottles of Ace of Spades champagne and heading upstairs to the VIP room, carrying his own duffle bags.

In the back of his mind he was worried that someone might have seen him hanging out the rear passenger's side window of Scrill's Bentley as he'd emptied his AK-47 into the Walkson brothers' Hummer, but he didn't really care that much. He'd beaten a ton of cases in the past. At the end of the day money talked, and he had more than enough to fight the case if he was charged.

He was on the top step, just about to turn and walk into VIP, when Cup appeared from the short hallway that led around a corner toward his office.

Out of the corner of his eye, he saw Meach reach in his duffle for his gun.

"I got that situation squared away," Cup said, holding a hand out for a shake as he approached Blake. "Found out that it was Mercedes all along."

"Yeah, I found out too," Blake said coldly. "What's up wit' all them threats, though? I don't take too kindly to that kinda shit."

"It was a misunderstanding, that's all. We're good now. Enjoy yourself. You see all the niggas I brought out? I got Kevin Gates and Chedda Da Connect in the building, too. Ross and Meek's here with Nicki. Got some bad ass strippers in the building. Let's have a good night."

Blake gritted his teeth as he shook Cup's hand. "Don't ever call me talking like that again, my nigga. Like I'm some hoe ass nigga or somethin'. You know this ain't that."

"My apologies." Cup nodded. "As I said, it was a simple misunderstanding. That bitch Mercedes tried to get us to fall out. I took care of it. Heard she's out of the picture for good, too, so there won't be any more of that."

"Next time call me and ask me if I did the shit. All that he say she say ain't on nothin'." Blake was tempted to take a swing at Cup, and he might have done it if he didn't see Lil Cholly stepping around the corner at that very moment.

"Go ahead and enjoy yourself in VIP," Cup said, opening the VIP's glass door. "I'll send up some special girls for you. We got some bad ones in the building tonight." He shook his head and licked his lips, as if the mere thought of the women made his mouth water.

Blake nodded and kept his eyes on Cup as he walked into the VIP section.

He took the table that — because of Blake himself — had become known as the "Baller's Table". It was right at the balcony that overlooked the stage where the strippers danced, and Cup always put the wealthiest person in VIP there to shower the strippers from above with cash.

One night not long ago, Blake had thrown nearly $500,000 down at Maliah as she'd worked the pole, and her eyes had stayed on him the entire time.

He looked over the balcony at all the club visitors and was surprised at what happened next.

First, Lil Wayne paused on stage and gave Blake a military-like salute.

"Shout out my nigga Bulletface, the biggest stunna ever, first billionaire in the game. We salute you, my nigga," Tunechi said.

And what followed was the biggest show of respect Blake had received thus far.

All over the nightclub's massive floor, people started looking up at Blake and giving their own salutations. Jeezy and Kevin Gates, who were already in VIP, stood up and gave their salutes as well.

A waitress rushed up the stairs with a microphone and handed it to Blake.

"Say something," she whispered in his ear. "The people love you." She paused and then added, "I love your fine ass, too."

He felt the peck of her soft lips on his cheek before she stepped aside and left him to speak.

The DJ cut the music.

"Tune, I salute you, too, big homie. To all the real niggas, stay trill, no matter the circumstances. Same to the bad bitches. Hold your niggas down when they get jammed up. Stay focused on gettin' some money and feedin' your families. Oh, and I can't forget, gotta salute the niggas who made this shit possible for a rap nigga like me, so R.I.P. to Pimp C, Pac, Biggie, and Eazy E. Shouts out to the whole NWA, make sure y'all check out that Straight Outta Compton when it hits theaters. Shout out Hove, Naz, Twista, Yo Gotti, Bump J, Kanye— every nigga that's influenced me in the rap game. I love this street shit, but family comes first, so take care of your people and get money. One hun'ed."

He handed the mic back to the waitress, who tried to lean in and kiss his cheek again but was immediately pushed away by Meach.

Wayne requested the DJ to play "Go DJ", and the club went haywire. There were three big-bootied strippers on the stage below; Blake popped the paper wraps on the bundles of hundreds he pulled from his pockets and began showering the girls with the crisp new Benjamins.

A line of waitresses carried Blake's bottles of Ace up to VIP with sparklers attached to them, but he only kept twenty of them and had the rest passed out to random people in the club.

He usually sipped his Lean and smoked his Kush, but tonight was a special night so he indulged in a bottle of the bubbly while his MBM team, Jeezy's CTE guys, King Louie's MUBU squad, and Rozay's MMG gang lit blunt after blunt of Kush and passed them around.

Blake felt invincible. He had singlehandedly ended the situation with T-Walk's brothers, and now Mercedes — one of the few people he'd wanted dead for the longest — was out of the picture as well, all thanks to Cup, the guy who'd gone from being an enemy to a friend.

He decided that it wouldn't hurt to let Cup live. Maybe he and Cup would make another $100 million or so in the dope game. After all, there was no such thing as too much money.

Chapter 34

When Mercedes came to she was in the backseat of a police car, her hands cuffed behind her, her head leaking profusely.

She raised up a few inches and looked at Porsche, who was lying next to her.

Porsche's eyes were open, but she wasn't moving.

Wincing as the back of her head throbbed with pain, Mercedes tried to remember what had happened. It took her a few seconds but eventually it came to her.

She'd gone to Cup's nightclub on Laramie and Chicago Avenue with the Walkson brothers trailing behind her Maybach. She and Porsche had walked into the club with Cup and Lil Cholly.

Nothing else came to mind.

She looked at Porsche again and would have screamed if not for the throbbing pain in her head.

Porsche was as stiff as a board.

Mercedes looked to the front seats. Two fat policemen were talking:

"The skinny one's dead for sure. Jesus Christ, how are we gonna get away with this?"

"Just calm down, will ya? There's nothing to worry about. You still got that gun you've always kept strapped to your ankle?"

"Of course I do. Got it off a prostitute back in '91, hasn't left my ankle since."

"We can put that on the other one. Shoot her sister with it and say she accidentally did it trying to kill us. We opened fire, killed her. Two dead chicks who were already in custody. Case dismissed."

"You see what happened with the Mike Brown incident in Missouri—"

"This is Chicago, not Ferguson. No one will question it. Just stick to your guns about this, alright? Let's get this handled first and then we'll go over our story. First we need to see if there's somewhere to just dump them. Look at their IDs and go with the story we gave Cup."

Mercedes's eyes widened in horror.

The officers were planning her murder, and according to them Porsche was already dead!

She wriggled her hands but it was to no avail; the handcuffs were on tight.

Then she felt her knuckles rub up against something soft.

She opened her hands and felt around behind her.

Her eyes widened again, only this time it was out of hope instead of fear.

Her purse was behind her.

There was a gun in her purse.

She shut her eyes and prayed as she struggled with the zipper, thinking that the zipper would get caught on something the way it sometimes did, but it opened without a hitch.

She dug in and seconds later her hands were wrapped around the butt of the gun.

Now what?

Wait, she told herself. Wait for the perfect opportunity and then turn and shoot. She'd blast right through the back of the seats and kill both of the crooked cops. Then she'd get Porsche to a hospital. Porsche couldn't be dead. Not her little sister. Porsche was all she had left. Without Porsche, the only living family Mercedes had left was Alexus and Pedro.

No, she had to save Porsche, and she had to do it now. Time was of the essence. If Porsche was badly hurt now she might die by the time Mercedes found the perfect opportunity to shoot the cops.

Taking several deep breaths, Mercedes waited for the car to come to a stop.

Then she made her move.

She sat up and recognized what street they were on. It was 73rd and Evans, just four blocks down from where her incarcerated uncle's wife stayed.

Swinging her hands around her left hip, she pulled the trigger.

BOOM! BOOM!

Two big holes appeared in the back of the driver's seat's head-rest, and the fat white cop behind the wheel slumped forward, the contents of his skull spraying out across the dashboard.

The car veered left and went speeding head on into a redbrick apartment building on the corner.

Mercedes saw the fear in the other policeman's eyes as she swung the gun around to her other hip and put four rounds through the back of his seat.

Then the car crashed into the building and spun out into the street with its hood open and smoking.

Mercedes was thrown every which way, and so was Porsche, but unlike the policemen Mercedes was conscious when the car came to a stop.

She shot out the window to her left, grabbed both her and Porsche's purses, and climbed out to the street.

A crew of young boys who'd been standing on the corner took off running.

"Wait!" Mercedes shouted, and winced as the back of her head started throbbing harder.

She watched the boys as they paused on the corner of 73rd and Cottage Grove and looked back at her.

Two of them came running back, but they stopped ten feet away and just stared.

"You shot them?" One of the boys asked.

"They were...trying...to do me like..Mike Brown." Every word hurt Mercedes's head. "Please just...get the cuff key. I'll pay...fifty thousand."

The two boys were both dark-skinned and thuggishly comported in dark colored t-shirts, jeans, and Nike Air Force One sneakers.

"She said $50,000, joe," one of the boys said to the other.

"Shit, come on." The second boy took off running toward the CPD squad car. He reached into the driver's window and shouted back, "Damn, they dead, broski! His brains all on the dash! Look like a envelope wit' some money in it, too!"

Suddenly their homies who'd taken off were running back to the corner. One of them helped Mercedes up and took her to the apartment building's front door. She slumped back against the steel-framed glass door and sighed. Tears came to her eyes.

"The girl...in the back!" she shouted, giving her head yet another splitting throb.

"She dead, too!" One of the boys shouted, and Mercedes broke down crying.

They removed the handcuffs and helped her into some old lady named Chief's second floor apartment. The elderly woman — one of the boy's grandmothers — was sitting in the living room in a threadbare easy chair when they burst inside.

Mercedes held the Gucci bags close to her chest until they had her in the bathroom. Then she set them on the toilet seat, but only long enough to rinse the blood from her head and face. The cool water made the pain more bearable. She looked in the mirror and saw a baseball-sized lump and a large gash on the rear left side of her head.

Mercedes was able to speak clearly, and the only thing on her mind was getting away with shooting the two policemen.

"Hurry and go clean up the blood from the hallway," she said, opening her purse to show them the bundles of cash she had. "Tell them the guy who jumped out ran whichever way. Somebody sow me up. Come on, now, let's get going."

Chapter 35

"Im back in charge. Fuck the bullshit," Alexus said as she paced a tight circle next to the Jacuzzi in her presidential suite at the resort, holding the goldplated, diamond-encrusted handle of her .50-caliber Desert Eagle in a death-grip and holding her iPhone 6 Plus and a glass of Hennessy in the other.

She took big gulps of the cognac.

Enrique was seated, typing furiously at the computer. He too had a glass of the cognac, only it was resting on a coaster next to him and not in his hand.

There were twenty-two Costilla Cartel militants in the suite with them, just a few of whom were drinking from their own glasses of Hennessy. Most of them were standing around in sharp white Armani suits with their submachine guns in hand, waiting for orders from the boss of all bosses — Alexus Costilla.

"Fuck," Enrique said. "It's a good thing you wore that mask at Gamuza's place. We need to get rid of the clothes you wore. Looks like Pedro's already uploaded that footage he recorded of you cutting off Gamuza's head to an online website."

"I did NOT fucking tell him to do that!" Alexus ranted. She screamed out in frustration and came very close to squeezing the Desert Eagle's trigger. Then she changed her mind and instead swallowed the remainder of her drink. "Call that motherfucker, Enrique. Call him right now and tell him I said to bring his ass to this suite. We need to have a serious fucking talk, and if he doesn't understand after this I'll send him to his conniving little college girl and let them both rest in peace."

Alexus was furious. Here she was, trying to be a good woman to her husband and child, even going as far as accepting Blake's daughter as her own, and what did she get in the end? A cheating-ass husband, and an ungrateful cousin.

"I see why Granny Costilla left everything to me!" Alexus said. "I'm the only real motherfucker in the mix!"

"Settle down. We're okay." Enrique turned in his chair and looked Alexus in the eyes. "Give the clothes you wore to one of our guys now. You'll be fine. Call Blake. You may be surprised. He might be actually telling you the truth."

Alexus rolled her eyes and moved them to her smartphone as she raised it to phone Blake. "Yeah the fuck right. He's fucking that whore. Nobody can tell me different. If she's there in Chicago with him, and he's buying her houses and all kinds of shit, they're fucking. I'm a woman. Trust me, I know these things."

The phone rang in her ear; she wasn't going to let Blake see her now, so a Facetime call was out of the question. She blamed it partly on the obvious guilt she knew would be in her eyes, and the other part she blamed on Blake not being worthy of seeing her again if he'd fucked Baddie Barbie.

She was both relieved and angry when it went to voicemail.

"He's fucking that bitch right now," Alexus said, teeth clenched together, nostrils flaring. "I'm killing that son of a bitch. Put out the order now, to every single one of the gangs we supply in the States. I want him dead. If I'm not with him—"

Alexus froze in place as her iPhone started vibrating and lit up with a call back from Blake.

She was spitting-mad when she answered.

"You nasty-dick ass nigga, I'm killing you for fucking that bitch!"

"What?! I ain't fucked nobody. Ask—"

"I'm not asking anybody!"

"Why would you not ask? Are you serious? You think I'd cheat on you and tell you about the shit? You drunk or somethin'?"

Alexus thought: Oh, shit. I'm drunk. Was I wrong? Did he really just put the girl in a better financial situation because he genuinely felt bad for making me go after her?

"Look, stop trippin' on me when I ain't did shit to make you feel that way. I just had to get down on T-Walk's brothers, damn near had to stank the nigga Cup. Shit crackin' out here in these streets. I'm supposed to have you to trust and love me like I trust and love you, 'cause these streets damned sure ain't gon' love me."

Alexus put down her glass and lifted a hand to her mouth as it fell open. Her eyes filled with tears. She'd fucked up royally by cheating with Enrique. Blake hadn't been fucking Barbie, as Alexus had initially assumed; she could hear the truth in his voice.

"What's wrong with you?" Blake asked. "You've been drinkin'. Don't even lie."

"A little bit." She bit the corner of her bottom lip and drew her shoulders in, suddenly hoping she could get away with her little misdeed. "I love yooooou."

"You crazy ass bitch," Blake said dryly.

Alexus snickered. "I know. You know how I be tripping over you. I'm crazy in love, Blakey."

"Now I'm Blakey." He put heavy emphasis on the 'now'. "I just stepped out in the hallway from VIP at The Visionary Lounge."

"Cup's nightclub in Chicago?"

"Hell yeah. Just reopened."

"I could've sworn you said y'all had beef."

"He squashed it. Said Mercedes was the reason for it. Speakin' of Mercedes, you might wanna check on her. He said he got her out the way. Her and Porsche."

"What do you mean? He's saying he killed them?"

"Fuck if I know. It's what it sounded like."

Alexus leaned her head to the side. "Oh, hell no. He's got me so fucked up. If something happened to my little sister I want that motherfucker dead."

"I'm not sure. I ain't seen Mercedes or Porsche since we first pulled up. I saw em pullin' up and gettin' out the Maybach, but I was too focused on T-Walk's brothers. Caught up with them down the avenue and tore that Hummer up."

"Are they...?"

"Shit, I hope so."

Just then another call came in on Alexus's smartphone.

It was from Mercedes's iPhone.

"Let me click over right quick. Looks like Mercedes calling."

"I'm about to leave the club, anyway. I'll hit you right back."

Alexus clicked over and immediately heard Mercedes sobbing through the phone. There was a strange buzzing sound in the background.

"What's going on?" Alexus asked.

It took Mercedes nearly a minute to reply: "Porsche's dead...I... think it was Lil Cholly. Somebody hit us from behind. He was the only one behind us at the time. Oh, my God, she was dead sitting next to me! She was already dead, Alexus! That nigga Cup! They hit us with somethin' in the back of our heads! Knocked us out! And some police were in on it!"

Now it was Alexus telling Mercedes to calm down. "You don't have to shout."

"I know. And it hurts my head so much. I just took some of this old lady's pain pills before I left."

"Left? Left where? Where are you?"

"On some kid's moped, riding down Cottage Grove with my head all wrapped up, hoping I don't get pulled over. About a hundred cop cars just sped past on their way to the scene. I had to shoot them to get away. Two cops, Alexus! I'm fucked!"

"No, you're fine. Get off that moped. You could have a concussion. Wouldn't want you passing out while riding it. Pay someone to drive you to the airport. I'll be there in three hours flat."

"No, I'm going back to get my car from in front of that club, and I'm going to make sure that nigga Cup sees me before I leave. This shit ain't over. Somebody has to go for my little sister."

"I'm on my way there, sis. Wait for me."

"Porsche's de—" Mercedes was saying as Alexus hit end and put the smartphone down on the coffee table next to her glass.

She looked at Enrique's smiling face.

"Blake wasn't cheating after all, huh?"

"They tried to kill my sister."

"Who's they?"

"Cup...and Lil Cholly. That guy he was always with. They hit Mercedes and Porsche in their heads with something and had some cops getting ready to finish their dirty work. At least that's what I gathered from the call."

"What about Blake? Does that order stand?"

Alexus smiled. "Of course it doesn't stand. We're fine now. Let's go to the airport."

Enrique put on a pout. "But what about me? Did I mean nothing to you?"

Alexus flipped him a middle finger and laughed. "Blake cheated on me, I got some payback. That's all It was. Don't take it personal."

Chapter 36

As soon as Blake got off the phone with Alexus he went back in VIP and got everyone ready to leave.

He had a gut feeling that he should leave now before Alexus sent a crew of Mexican gangsters into the club to deal with Cup.

The strippers hugged him tightly when he made it down the stairs; he'd thrown $300,000 in hundred-dollar bills down on them, which was much more than the average rainmaker made fall from the sky. One of the girls slid him a phone number, and she sent the others rushing to find ink pens so they could do the same thing before he left. Three more of the girls managed to push pieces of paper in his pockets as he was walking out the rear door.

In the parking lot he faced a dilemma: they had all arrived in Scrill's Bentley, and they'd used it in the shooting on Chicago Avenue.

Blake refused to get in it.

"Fuck that," he said, looking around the dark parking lot.

He spotted a woman in a dark dress walking toward a gray newer-model Camaro. She had a similar looking friend stumbling along behind her, and her eyes were on Blake.

"Bulletface?!" she shouted.

Blake looked back at the gang and motioned for them to follow him. He ran to the woman, and she hugged him just as tightly as the strippers had and introduced herself as Shalonda.

"Can we ride with you?" Blake asked. "You know money ain't shit to me, I'll pay you."

"Boy, that ain't even a question," she said, opening her door. "Get in. Somebody gotta put my sis on their lap. Bulletface, you sit in the front with me."

"Ain't that a bitch?" Meach said with a chuckle. "She ain't sittin' on my lap."

The girl ended up on Scrill's lap in the backseat. Blake tried to decide how much he'd pay Shalonda for the ride. Sometimes it wasn't good to give away too much. People were starting to expect him to be overly generous.

But since Shalonda was quite possibly keeping him from catching a murder case, he said fuck it and gave her a packet of hundreds.

She stuffed it in her bra and drove to the parking lot's entrance.

"Don't go down Chicago Avenue," Blake said. "Turn left. We'll take Laramie down a few blocks first, then you can turn whichever way you want to."

Shalonda did as she was told. She turned up the volume on MBM's latest mixtape. Blake rolled his window down and listened, nodding his head to the beat as his verse began on the remix to Meach's "Coke Girl". It featured French Montana and Lil Durk.

'I need me a coke girl, I got me a coke girl
Hope she can bring me all the kilograms in the whole world
This bitch want some bread from me
You know I'm like no girl
This bitch want some head from me
You know I'm like no girl

Ol' girl...say she wanna fuck
I said I wanna whip
She say "what you whippin'?"
I say bitch this here's a half a brick
She smiled and laughed and shit
Passed the spliff, like boy yo ass a trip
Then she sucked me up so fuckin good
I damn near crashed the whip
Promise I ain't lyin'
When you see her you can ask the bitch
Her Papi had the bricks
He fucked wit' me 'cause of my master whip
Plus, I was already ballin' pushin Jags and shit
Slangin' whole thangs and half a bricks
Right off the Ave. and shit
First time I laid eyes on her
Man, all I saw was ass and tits

Then she showed me the cash and bricks
I never had to ask for shit...'

Shalonda lowered the music volume and turned to Blake with a nervous look on her face. They had just passed two police cars that were speeding in the opposite direction.

"Did y'all do something?" Shalonda asked.

"I ain't did shit. My car broke down," Blake said. "We needed a ride. Is that against the law?"

"Just asking. They say two boys got shot up real bad on Chicago Avenue. And two cops just got killed on the south side, so you know they ain't gon' be playin' no games tonight." She picked up a CD case that went to the mixtape she was playing. "Y'all mind signing this for me?"

"No problem. Let's get us to the crib first. It's a condo in Lincoln Park."

"That's cool."

In the back seat, Meach said, "Maaaan, if this girl throw up on me it's gon' be somethin'."

Shalonda laughed. "That's my sister, y'all. She's good. Just got a lil too drunk, that's all. They gave us one of those bottles of Ace y'all bought and she drank that shit like water, on top of the Ciroc she had already had when we first got to the club. Man, it was packed in there, wasn't it? I can't believe I got to take a picture with Rick Ross! Wait until I show my daughter, she gon' kill me."

"You got a daughter that's old enough to know who Ross is?" Blake was surprised. He'd guessed Shalonda's age to be no more than 25.

"Hell yeah, boy, I'm thirty-four," she said. "My oldest daughter is eighteen. Ooh, she is really going to throw a fit when I tell her I actually had you in my passenger seat. Knowing her freaky ass she'll probably ask why I didn't try nothin'."

She batted her eyes at Blake, and he grinned. He wasn't trying to go there, though he could tell that Shalonda was more than ready.

Just then, one of his iPhones rang.

It was Alexus, saving the day.

"I'm on the way to—" he said when he answered.

"No! Go back to the club! My sister's going back to the club!" There was panic and fear in Alexus's voice.

"Baby, baby...calm the fuck down and talk to me like you got some sense. What are you talkin' about?"

Shalonda gasped and silently mouthed, "Alexus?"

Blake nodded and held up a finger for her to hold on while Alexus talked.

"You were right," Alexus said. "They tried to kill her. Cup and that nigga Lil Cholly. They killed Porsche and had some cops getting ready to get rid of the bodies but Mercedes shot them and got away. She's on her way back to The Visionary Lounge, Blake. I need you to be there to stop her from doing something stupid. She'll get herself killed out there."

Blake paused to think. They were only about four or five minutes away from Mocha's condo where his Bugatti was parked. He knew he'd be able to make it back to the club in record time.

"You gotta give me like fifteen minutes, baby. I'll be back there by then."

"I'm on my plane, Blake. Don't let anything happen to her."

"I gotchoo."

"Okay, we're taking off now. I'll be there in two hours and forty-five minutes."

"Okay. Love you."

"Love you more," Alexus said, and ended the call.

Shalonda went right in. "Oh, my God, that was Alexus! Shit! She can afford to buy this whole damn city!" She stopped at a red light on Division and leaned toward Blake with her smartphone raised for a selfie.

Chapter 37

Mercedes had to stop several times as she was struck by brief spells of dizziness. Maybe she did have a concussion, but she wasn't going to let it stop her from returning to the nightclub where her Maybach was parked.

She wondered where V-Walk and B-Walk were at. She'd called their phones twice already and had gotten no answers.

The pain pills she'd taken had her feeling numb. She had just turned onto Chicago Avenue, but she was still far away from The Visionary Lounge. She had about twenty-five blocks to go before she made it to Laramie.

There were police cars everywhere.

Mercedes silently hoped that the Walkson brothers had finally gotten to Blake.

She pulled over at a gas station to fill up the moped's tank and ran into a pair of handsome light-skinned twin brothers named Demont and Demone. They were in a silver Cadillac on big chrome rims.

She talked to them in the gas station and they offered to give her a lift to her car once they realized that she was Mercedes Costilla. She gave the moped to a teenager who'd stopped by the gas station for blunts and got in the Cadillac with the twins.

"Damn, what the fuck happened to your head?" Demone asked as he looked back at her from the passenger seat.

"It's a long story." Mercedes's voice was as dry as her throat felt from riding the moped for so long. She took a swig of the Pepsi she'd gotten at the gas station. "Go to The Visionary Lounge. My car's parked right out front."

"We just left from there," Demone said. "Nigga, they had everybody in that bitch tonight. I took a picture with Nicki. Wanted to grab her ass but that nigga Meek was there. Damn, wish I would've seen you. Ask bro, I always said I'd rather fuck you than any other celebrity. You from right here in the city, and that ass you got is real. At least I think it is."

"There's nothing fake on me," Mercedes said when she realized he was waiting on a response.

"I knew that shit. Bruh thought you had a fake ass and fake titties. I showed this nigga some old school pictures I found of you online. That ass been there."

"It sure has." Mercedes took the Glock pistol out of Porsche's Gucci handbag and set it on her lap.

Demone looked at the gun, and for a moment he said nothing; then, "What's that for? You don't see all these muhfuckin cops out here? If we get pulled over don't try to throw that muhfucka on the floor. We're on federal probation. They'll give us all day for that shit."

The other twin looked back from the driver's seat. "Damn, lil mama with the shits, too." He laughed. "I heard Alexus was the same way. They say she got like ten bodies."

"Ten?" Mercedes scoffed at the low number. She'd been in Mexico once with Alexus and watched the Costilla Cartel's soldiers murder over a hundred men and women on Alexus's orders. "Alexus is my blood sister, and even I'm scared of her. She's the craziest bitch since Griselda Blanco. I don't even like being around her."

"Shit," Demone said, stretching out the word, "I would gladly live with that bad muhfucka. We used to think you and her was twins like us. What's up with your sister Porsche? Whatever happened to the sex tape she had with Bulletface? They still ain't released that muhfucka yet."

Mercedes struggled to hold back the tears. "I don't wanna talk about her. Just drop me off. Please. I'd appreciate it."

"Can I get your number?" Demone asked.

Mercedes gritted her teeth. "A pretty boy like yourself, you don't need my number. I'm sure you're fucking half the thots in this city."

"Nah, hell nah. That ain't me. That's bruh. I'm the laid back one."

What Mercedes wanted to say was, "I really don't give two fucks who you or your brother is fucking or have fucked, just shut up and get me to the club before I put a hole in your ass!"

Instead, she said, "Hold on. Let me send out this text. I can't talk and text at the same time."

She went to her text messages and sent a meaningless text to herself. Demone watched her, eagerly waiting for his chance to speak again.

Mercedes wanted to choke him.

Luckily, the Cadillac made it to the club just seconds later, and Mercedes pushed open her door and got out hurriedly.

It seemed like everyone was leaving the club. A few pairs of eyes studied the gauze bandage that was wrapped around her head. She checked the driver's seat of her shiny black Maybach and saw that Shakema was gone. She dialed Shakema's number and leaned against the door with the smartphone to her ear, glowering across the street at the club's front door with Porsche's handbag sitting open on the hood.

She thought: If Cup or Lil Cholly come walking out of that door I'm shooting. No questions asked. They deserve every bullet in the fucking clip.

Shakema picked up. "Girl, where the fuck are you? I've been looking everywhere for you and Porsche."

"Where you at now?"

"I'm in the bathroom."

"In the club?"

"Of course I'm in the club. Where the hell else I'ma be? I'm on the toilet taking a piss. I came in here looking for you and Porsche."

"Have you seen Cup? Or Lil Cholly?"

"Yeah. They're on the floor, thanking the guests for coming or something. Girl, did you hear what happened to those boys y'all went to the movies with?"

Mercedes knitted her brows. Demone got out of the Cadillac and tried walking up to her, but she put an arm out, gesturing for him to stay back.

Two girls that were crossing the street laughed, and one of them shouted, "Haaaa! Demone, she just lamed yo' lame ass. Give her fifty feet, nigga."

He went to arguing with both of the girls, calling them dirty, dusty, and all kinds of other, more derogatory names, and then three girls that were on the opposite corner made claims that the twins were their cousins and the two girls had Demone fucked up.

Shakema went on. "Somebody put about a hundred bullets in that Hummer, and I'm not exaggerating. I saw it for myself when I drove down there to get somethin' to eat from McDonald's, and I stayed there and watched until the police had it on the tow truck. Everybody swears they didn't see shit but Kathy — you remember Kathy, off Chicago Avenue and St. Louis, Lemonhead's baby mama — she said Money Bagz did it. I'm guessing she means Blake and his crew."

"Stay in the bathroom. I'm on my way in now, and trust me you don't want any parts of what's about to go down."

"Wait, what?!"

Mercedes ended the call and started off across the street with her hand in the Gucci bag. She'd washed her own gun off and given it to the youngsters who'd helped her on the south side, but she didn't need it. Porsche's 30-round clip was more than enough firepower. Even if she was shot down while trying to get at Cup, it would be worth it. In the name of her little sister, Mercedes was willing to die.

The girls on the corner started fighting over the remarks made about Demone. Mercedes guessed that he was probably fucking one of the trio and not really related to either of them. She'd used that excuse many times in the past when she wanted to whoop a bitch's ass in the hood and couldn't find an excuse to do it.

Tears formed in her eyes as she was in the middle of the street, making her way toward the door.

She was stopped in her tracks by a flawless white sports car as it came to a screeching halt directly in front of her.

First she noticed that the car was a Bugatti Veyron Grand Sport.

Then she noticed that its driver was none other than Blake "Bulletface" King.

King Rio

Chapter 38

"Hold on one second. I know what happened, a'ight? Just wait for bruh to pull up," Blake said as he stepped out of the Bugatti with his large duffle bag in hand.

The duffle was unzipped, and inside it was the compact AK-47 that had not been used in the Walkson murders; the one he'd used had already been wiped down and ditched in a west side alley-way.

Meach veered around the corner in his Lamborghini and parked right behind Blake's car. He climbed out holding his own Louis Vuitton duffle bag, only inside his were two .40-caliber Glocks with 50-round drums.

Blake looked around and saw no police in the area. He was tempted to watch the girl brawl that was going down in the parking lot of an abandoned McDonald's that sat catercorner from the night-club but the situation with Cup took precedence over the girlfight.

He took a deep breath and walked to the glass double-doors at the front of the nightclub with Meach and Mercedes.

But just as Meach was getting ready to snatch open the door, and as Blake was about to pull out the AK-47 and enter the club on some gangster shit, two cop cars pulled up to the corner from off Laramie and parked.

All four of the policemen immediately looked at Blake, as if they already knew where he'd be standing when they hit the corner.

"Change of mothafuckin plans, nigga," Meach said as he let go of the door and put on a show as if he was chucking up the deuces to someone in the club. He walked back to his car.

Blake canceled his plan to join Mercedes in the club and instead tossed his duffle in through the Bugatti's passenger window as he walked around to the driver door.

Mercedes became frozen in place, but only for a couple of seconds.

Blake inhaled deeply as Mercedes pulled the gun and rushed inside the club. Before the door closed behind her, she drew her Glock handgun and opened fire.

Chapter 39

Mercedes saw Lil Cholly first.

He was standing in a circle of scantily clad women with a black bottle of Belaire Rosé in one hand and the crotch of his slacks in the other, smiling brightly as one woman stroked a hand across his jawline.

She turned on the Glock pistol's red laser sighting as she dropped the Gucci handbag and took aim at him.

The first bullet went through the jawline stroker's forearm and pierced the left side of Cholly's chest. Mercedes sent the second shot with the assistance of the red dot, and the bullet skewered his throat.

Lil Cholly slapped a hand to the gushing wound and hit the floor...just as Cup's crew of Travelers, Breeds, 4 Corner Hustlers, and some more guys from his Lawndale neighborhood pulled their guns.

Mercedes saw Cup standing off to the side of his crew a second before they opened up on her with a barrage of gunfire.

Ducking low, she put the red dot on Cup's head and was just able to pull the trigger twice before she was gunned down.

Mercedes got the chance to see one of her bullets hit Cup right in the center of his forehead before she fell dead to the floor.

Chapter 40

The Bugatti could not go fast enough.

Bold statement, seeing that the car went up to speeds of 250 miles-per-hour, but as Blake pressed the pedal to the floor on the highway, veering around other vehicles as he raced to the airport, he didn't feel like he was going as fast as he was.

There was a Styrofoam cup of Lean in his right hand, a blunt of Kush burning between the tips of his index and middle fingers. He had the AK-47 laying on his duffles in the passenger seat.

Behind him Scrill and Biggs were struggling to keep up in the Ferrari he'd bought for Biggs two years ago, and behind them was Meach in the Lamborghini.

Meach made a Facetime call to Blake: "Bruh, slow down before the law get on our trail. Damn, you got a Bugatti, nigga. Ease up on that pedal."

Blake realized the risk he was taking flying down the highway at such high speeds and slowed to just under 90 miles-per-hour.

He was right on time.

An Illinois State Trooper came racing by mere seconds later.

"I'm tryna hurry up and get to wifey before she fuck around and lose her mind." Blake hit the blunt. "You know most of her family's been killed, just like mine. She was already trippin' over Mercedes. That's why we slid on the club in the first place."

"Ain't no need to trip over Mercedes no more," Meach said matter-of-factly. "You heard all them shots. Ain't no way in hell she made it through that shit."

Blake had no choice but to acknowledge that what Meach was saying was more than likely the truth of the matter. Blake had seen the blasts of gunfire through The Visionary Lounge's front doors as he'd peeled off down Chicago Avenue. In his rearview, he'd seen the policemen rushing out of their vehicles and into the tall yellow-stone building.

Mercedes was most definitely a very dead woman. There wasn't a doubt on Blake's mind that she'd succumbed to a number of gunshot wounds during her entrance into the club.

He smoked his blunt, discarded it out his window, and put fire to another one. He had nine missed calls in his phone, mostly from the rap artists he'd bumped into at the club, but he was in no mood to negotiate music deals at the moment. He was far too worried about his wife.

It took Blake less than ten more minutes to reach the airport. Alexus's Gulfstream 650 jet had just landed when Blake and the gang perambulated out onto the tarmac, boarding a black Range Rover that took them straight to the bottom stair next to the private jet as Alexus hurriedly descended the stairs.

She ran right into Blake's arms as soon as he got out of the Rover.

"I just read about a shooting at The Visionary Lounge. Were you involved? Are you okay?"

She took a step back and held Blake's face in her hands.

He almost couldn't tell her.

"It's...Mercedes," he said finally, his hands rubbing her lower back. "She ran in and started shootin'. Cops was right there. I couldn't help without gettin' jammed up myself."

Meach rolled down his window and backed Blake's statement. "He ain't lyin', sis. On Angelo, we was just about to go live from hell in that thang, you feel me? Law pulled down and got us out the way."

Gazing into Blake's eyes, Alexus pressed her lips against his and held them there for a long while. When she pulled back there were tears in her beautiful green eyes.

Enrique's smartphone was ringing as he walked down the stairs behind Alexus; he answered and spoke for a couple of seconds, then tapped Alexus on the shoulder.

She turned to him, and he gave her a somber nod of the head.

"Noooooo!" Alexus screamed.

She collapsed against Blake and sobbed for a full ten minutes before he was able to walk her back up the stairs and into the jet.

Dropping down in a seat and pulling Alexus onto his lap, Blake told Enrique to head for Miami Beach.

At a time like this, the only thing that could console him and his wife was being with their children.

King Rio

Chapter 41

The kids were fast asleep when Alexus and Blake made it home to the Versace Mansion in Miami Beach, Florida.

But the grownups were wide awake.

Rita, Britney, and Dr. Melonie Farr were sitting in the family room watching the news of Mercedes Costilla's murder on CNN and drinking from crystal stem glasses of red wine.

Neither of them stood or said a word as Alexus walked in with Blake shadowing her, his arms wrapped tight around her slender waistline. Enrique, Sergio, Meach, Scrill, and Biggs followed them into the family room.

Everyone cast intense stares at the television as Anderson Cooper delivered the heartbreaking news:

'Porsche Clark and Mercedes Costilla have both been killed in separate incidents in Chicago tonight. Another man — known throughout Chicago as one of its most prominent business owners — was also killed in the nightclub shootout that claimed the life of Mercedes. Police are still investigating but from the looks of it the club shooting is connected to a south Chicago shooting that claimed the lives of two CPD officers. According to various reports, Mercedes Costilla walked into The Visionary Lounge, a popular Chicago nightclub owned by the businessman who was also murdered, firing a pistol at him and a close friend of his. Both men were killed. Members of the businessman's entourage then opened fire on Mercedes, killing her.

'Apparently, American billionaire Alexus Costilla wasn't involved in either incident, despite the steady flow of legal troubles she herself faces on what seems like a monthly basis. Her husband — the man known as Hip Hop's very first billionaire, rapper Bulletface — has also been cleared by the Chicago Police Department of any involvement, though he was reportedly seen racing away from the scene of the club shooting '

"Well," Rita said as she stood up and hugged Alexus. "At least this time your name's not in it. What was Mercedes thinking? She could have easily become a successful businesswoman. Why would she go into that club and start shooting like that?"

Alexus shrugged her shoulders and went to crying again. The feel of Blake's lips on the nape of her neck relaxed her, and the firm grip of his hands on her hips was even more soothing.

She heard his whisper at her right ear: "I love you, my queen. Just be strong, a'ight. If you ain't got nobody you got me and God. That's all we need, baby. Just God, us, and the kids."

His loving words forced the tears out of her eyes and sent them skiing down her face. Rita dabbed them away with a Kleenex.

Getting up from her seat on the sofa, Dr. Farr said, "Come to my office for a twenty minute session." She grabbed ahold of Alexus's wrist, and Blake let her go.

In the second-floor office, Alexus fell back onto the big white leather sofa across from Dr. Melonie Farr's desk, crossed her arms over her face, and cried.

It took a few minutes for Farr's soft voice to violate the silence.

"Mercedes is in a better place now, Alexus. She's with her mom, her dad, her children, her children's father...her little sister."

"Papi told me to look after her right before he died," Alexus said with a loud sniffle. "It's all he asked."

"It was in God's will for her to go now. You can't blame yourself for this, okay? Mercedes was a grown woman, just a year younger than you are. She lived, she loved...she experienced life. It was her decision to walk in that club and shoot those men. You can't fault yourself for this. You had nothing to do with it. Be grateful that your husband wasn't killed. Be grateful that you and your children are still fine and healthy. There's no need in dwelling on things you have no control over. Think about the things you do have control over, like the future of your marriage, and the future of your little ones. Concentrate on that. I know you're going to grieve, but don't beat yourself up at the same time. What you need to be doing is putting on your best lingerie and giving your husband the loving he needs before you two go to bed, because both of you are lost, in my opinion. Neither of you truly know the meaning of love. You've got all the money in the world, but without God you have nothing. If I were you, I'd be taking my butt to church first thing tomorrow and learning how to work out the differences between me and my husband before it's too late, before the same evil that just took Mercedes under pries its way into your love life."

Alexus ruminated over what Melz had just said for a long while. During this time her tears dried, and her hands balled into fists.

"You know what?" Alexus sat up and then stood. "You are absolutely right. I've messed up, Blake has messed up — hell, we've all messed up. But in the end I still have him. He needs my loving just as much as I need his. How weak am I to be lying here crying like a baby when he could have easily lost his life out there today? I'm supposed to be his backbone at times like this, his rock."

"You see," Melonie said, standing up and smiling, "that's the Alexus Costilla that hired me. I don't know where this weak bitch comes in but you really need to cancel her visitation rights because the Alexus I know can handle anything. Am I right or wrong?"

"You're right." Alexus smiled and thumbed away the tears. "That weak bitch's visiting rights are officially revoked. From here on out I'll be the strongest Black and Mexican woman the world has ever seen."

Chapter 42

Blake was stretched out in bed, watching Sportscenter in his boxers and smoking a blunt, when Alexus crept into their bedroom. He glanced at her as she locked the door, put her Chanel bag on the dresser, and sauntered into the bathroom.

"You a'ight, baby?" he asked.

"Yeah, I'm fine. I talked to Melz. She set me straight. I was trippin' a little, but I'm back now?"

"How far back? Like, all the way back?"

"Yeah. All the way. I'm alright now."

"You mean like sit on this dick and make my night right right?"

Alexus let out a laugh. "Yes, Blake. I'm here for us. Just promise me one thing."

"Your wish is my command." Blake sat up, intrigued.

"Promise me that you'll never cheat on me with Barbie, Bubbles, Nona, or any other bitch. Ever again. I mean it."

"Baby, I promise." Blake got up and traced her steps into the bathroom. He found her sitting in a tub full of warm, bubbly water. He remembered watching her text the mansion staff ahead of time while they were getting off the plane to let them know that she wanted her bath water ready when she got home.

It was still lukewarm.

Blake sat on the edge of the tub and kissed her lips while she soaped herself clean.

"I'm sorry for tripping on you so much," she said, her tone as soft as cotton. "It's just that I love you so much and I don't ever want to live without you. You're all I've ever wanted in a man. Without you, I don't know what I'd do. And I mean that."

Blake kissed her again. Then he took off his jewelry, put it all on the sink, and stepped into the shower.

He thought of the repercussions that were certain to arise from Cup's death and then shrugged it off. He figured God had carried him this far. There was nothing he feared in his future after having gone through complete hell in his past. With Gamuza, Cup, the Walkson brothers, Porsche, and Mercedes gone, he didn't really have any enemies left. He doubted if the associates of the dead men and women would avenge their deaths; more than likely they'd mourn them for a short while and then move on, just like everyone else did when they lost friends and family.

Blake's face was covered in soap, and his eyes were shut when he heard the glass shower door opening and closing.

He heard her in his ear: "I forgive you for everything you've ever done since we got married."

"You mean that?" he asked.

"Of course I do," Alexus replied.

"Tell me everything I need to forgive you for and I'll tell you the same."

"Oh, please. I don't wanna hear about your trifling whore stories and I'm sure you don't want to hear mine."

Blake rinsed off the soap and grinned at Alexus's perfect brown face. "Who else have you fucked? Other than T-Walk?"

He received a tight stare for the question.

"Damn, it's that serious?" he said, chuckling and squeezing her meaty butt in both of his strong hands.

"Him and one more person. Okay? Now you tell me who all you've slept with."

"I don't believe that shit. You fucked more than one nigga."

"No, I actually didn't."

"Who was it?"

"Give me your whore stories first," Alexus demanded, planting her hands on her hips.

Blake slapped his hands on her ass and moved forward until her back was pressed to the glass wall. He kissed her, passionately, lovingly, rubbing on her ass and putting the full weight of his chest against her breasts.

His phallus grew hard within seconds.

Alexus jerked it in her hands as she returned his kiss.

"You're right," he said. "I apologize. No matter the number of bitches I fucked, the number should be zero. I'm wrong, you're wrong, and that's that. But I swear on my soul I didn't cheat on you today. I haven't cheated ever since I was with Nona in Hawaii, and I'll never do it again. That's my word."

Alexus smiled at him for almost a minute before she began to urgently scrub his body down.

It didn't take a rocket scientist to see that she was hungry for him.

He felt the same way about her.

When she made it to his twelve-inch love muscle, she held it in her hands and stroked it gently, gazing up into his eyes.

Anxious to feel her touch, Blake nearly slipped and fell as they got out of the shower.

He rushed putting on his deodorant. Alexus lotioned him down, and she took her sweet time rubbing the lotion on his dick. He did the same to her, taking longer than necessary to lotion up her breasts and plump buttocks.

By the time they made it back to bed, his dick was as hard as a baseball bat, jutting out from his groin and swaying from side to side.

Alexus lay down on her back, sitting up on a pillow, and motioned for him with an indeed finger, biting her bottom lip and digging a finger in her pussy.

She stirred the finger around, and the sopping wet sound it made drove Blake crazy.

He leaned down over her and gave her another passionate kiss.

"I love you so much, Alexus. You gotta start trusting me."

"We need to start going to church," she replied breathlessly. "I want this love forever."

"And so do I."

Blake pushed the head of his oversized pole into her and forced it in deep.

Her mouth dropped open.

Her fingernails dug in his back.

It was a feeling he'd never forget.

He sank his dick in as far as it would go and started pumping, in and out, slowly at first but then quicker, much quicker.

Alexus began moaning. Loud moans that were guaranteed to be heard if they didn't do something about it.

Easing out of her, Blake grabbed the Smart television's remote control, went to his latest mixtape on iTunes, and hit play. He turned the volume up until all he heard was his music blasting from the surround sound speakers.

Lucky for him, the first song was the only one on the whole mixtape that was dedicated to Alexus. It was a slow track, featuring Trey Songz.

Blake took the nipple of his wife's left breast in his mouth and twirled his tongue all around it as he went back to fucking her senseless. All she could do was stare up at him with her mouth wide open, gasping and moaning at his every thrust. He shoved in as much as possible every forward stroke, because he liked how it made her mouth and eyes open wider each time.

When he pushed her legs up a few minutes later, he was surprised to see her sink the tip of an index finger in her asshole.

She saw the shock register on his face.

"Put it in there," she said.

Blake couldn't remember ever putting his dick in Alexus's ass but he wasn't about to turn it down. Right now, as beautiful and thick as Alexus was looking, she could've asked him to put his dick in her ear and he'd have agreed.

He was just easing the head in when she her eyes went really wide, almost as wide as her butthole stretched to accommodate his huge phallus.

And here he was hit with yet another surprise: Alexus could take it. He'd never thought she would be able to handle him there but she did, pulling his face down to hers so that she could bite and suck on his lips as he fucked her where he'd never fucked her before.

The tightness of it made Blake pull out mere seconds later. He had to regroup before he came too soon.

He turned her over on all fours and she backed up until his dick was sandwiched between her extra meaty buttocks.

He went right back into the forbidden hole, biting the middle of his bottom lip, kneading her fluffy cheeks in his powerful dark hands. He thought of all the millions of people — both men and women — who were so obsessed with his wife's beauty that they regularly posted heart-eyed emojis under all her Instagram photos and wore shirts and dresses with her image on the front.

The woman all those people lusted after was his woman.

Blake's grin stretched wider than her asshole.

Just a few minutes later the snugness became too much. Blake yanked out and shot his load across her ass as she twisted her hips and made her butt bounce and jiggle, looking back over her shoulder at him.

He fell down next to her onto his side of the bed. She got up and went to the bathroom with ropes of semen dangling from her ass and sliding down between her thighs. When she returned seconds later the cum was gone. She wiped his deflating pole clean with two wet wipes and then lay down next to him with her head on his shoulder, staring lovingly at the side of his face while he flipped through the channels, finally landing on Katt Williams' "It's Pimpin', Pimpin'".

"This that one from 2008," Blake said with a laugh. "Poor lil Tink-Tink." He laughed again.

"I love you so much, Blake."

"I love you even more. Damn, I married your crazy ass. That had to be love."

"Oh, shut up. I am not crazy. If anything you made me go crazy a few times, fucking with those bitches."

"I swear on my life it'll never happen again. Didn't I tell you that already?"

"I know...but it still kinda pisses me off when I think about it. This dick belongs to me and only me." Alexus grabbed his dick for emphasis. "I don't ever want another bitch to know how good it feels. I should cut this motherfucker off."

"You should get the fuck off me talkin' that kinda shit." Grinning, Blake turned and put a soft kiss on Alexus's forehead. "You ain't gotta worry about me ever fucking another woman for as long as we're married. I'm hoping that's until we're old and gray."

"Awww." She kissed his shoulder. "I promise to be just as faithful."

"You still ain't told me who that other nigga is you fucked."

"I'm taking that one to the grave with me."

"Ain't that a bitch?!" Blake laughed and shook his head, but the secret didn't bother him. He had cheated on her and she had cheated on him. As long as she kept it a hundred from here on out, he was content.

"We're starting church this Sunday," she said. "My mom's old church in your hometown is finished being renovated. I think we should go every Sunday from now on. It'll be good for the kids, and it'll put more money in your neighborhood. We can set up all kinds of programs for the kids in the community. Good after school programs, you know, so they won't have to be out there selling drugs like you were when we first met."

"What about the cartel?" Blake asked.

"What about it? Pedro's turning into a snake already but he'll run things for now. I don't want anything more to do with it, although I almost decided on moving back when I thought you and that bitch were in Chicago fucking again. Now that Gamuza's dead, I don't have anything else to prove. I feel like I did the one thing my father and grandmother wanted done. I got the payback my family deserved." She went silent for a moment. "I kinda feel bad about killing Pedro's little college girl, but that bitch was a snake, too. She tried to get Pedro to turn on me."

"Damn, you killed Mary?"

Alexus didn't reply. She changed the subject. "Mercedes and Cup are dead now, so at least you don't have to keep living knowing the man responsible for kidnapping Vari and killing her mom is no longer breathing, and my sister won't be trying to set you up anymore."

"I guess that's a good way of lookin' at it." He pulled her on top of him and slapped his hands down onto her thighs.

"Ouch!" She slapped his chest. "That hurt, you black bastard."

"Not as much as my heart hurts."

She squinted at him. "And why exactly is your heart hurting?"

"I could've been fuckin' you in the ass, and you're just now letting me do it. Took me five years." Blake acted as if he was getting ready to cry.

Alexus rolled her eyes and gave his chest another slap.

"Seriously," she said. "We're going to stay together and make this work. I'm sorry for getting mad at you earlier. I have to learn to trust you more. I just had a nice little talk with Melonie, and she set me straight."

"I'm here forever, baby," Blake said, the palms of his hands roaming the swells of her derrière. "I ain't going nowhere."

For a moment Alexus gazed down at him, caressing his bulging pectoral muscles as he rubbed her ass and thighs. His dick grew hard underneath her. She guided it into her juicy nookie and gave her husband the ride of his life.

Epilogue
Nine Months Later...

The people of Mexico City became used to seeing the dozen or more white Rolls-Royce Phantoms rolling back to back through the city within weeks after Pedro Costilla moved there.

He found a new girlfriend, an 18-year-old African American girl from Brooklyn named Alana. She was a runway model from the ghetto. Pedro called it the perfect combination. He'd taken her to the gun range on their very first date and taught her how to properly and efficiently use handguns and assault rifles.

Sitting across from him at the dinner table one night at his seventy-million-dollar hilltop mansion, Alana said, "It's kind of weird that you run this great big empire yet you could be pushed aside at any given moment if and when Alexus ever decides to return."

Pedro shook his head. "You might not want to say that. My last girlfriend lost her head for saying that."

"Lost her head?"

"She got killed for talking against Alexus."

"Really? Wow." Alana sank her teeth into a crab cake. "Sorry. You shouldn't have told me about Alexus running things when you were drinking last night. I tend to give my opinion when I'm told something as crazy as that. You know, for a while I thought the rumors that Alexus was the boss of the Matamoros drug cartel were false. Even when she was indicted for allegedly running the cartel I swore up and down that she was being set up by the government because she's a Black woman with so much money. And when the charges were dropped I won a twenty-dollar bet off my mom, who just knew for sure that Alexus was going down."

Pedro pushed back from the table and stood, dabbing a napkin across his mouth. He donned a white Gucci suit with a white-and-gold tie and pocket square. His rose gold Rolex watch twinkled in the light of the crystal chandeliers that hung from the high ceiling.

He filled a stem glass with his favorite wine and crossed the room to one of the floor to ceiling windows at the east wall of his hilltop palace.

From this vantage point he could see many of the city lights shining bright in the distance. It was late, a quarter to midnight.

"This isn't my destiny, Alana," he said, pouring the cool wine in his mouth. "I'm supposed to be the number-one boss in all of Mexico. Second place is for losers. Mary was right. I should've killed Alexus when I had the chance. She's nine months pregnant with an American rap star's baby right now, yet she's still sending orders through Enrique. She sends orders without even talking things over with me. She continues to take millions of dollars in profits that are supposed to come to me. A few months back, she even had the audacity to cancel a hit I'd ordered on an FBI agent in the States for prying too much into the family business."

He paused, gritting his teeth and shaking his head. He watched Alana's reflection as she walked up behind him and then kept staring out the window.

"But I've got a plan," he went on, talking more to himself than to Alana. "There's something I'm working on that'll end all these attempts they've been making to leave me powerless here in my country."

"What kind of plan, Pedro? Let me hear it." Alana spoke in the dull tones people used when they believed the person they were speaking to was making a terrible mistake.

"El Chapo. He's the key. He's the one man I can go to who wants Alexus out of power just as badly as I do. He just broke out of prison. His cartel — the Sinaloas — they still have some of Mexico in their grasp, but it's nowhere near the amount of land and people they had before Alexus became boss."

"I can't believe I'm actually talking to someone who knows El Chapo." Alana shook her head.

"He and I will go into business in the coming months. We'll work out a deal to get rid of Alexus, and I'll end up with the position I deserve," Pedro said.

Just then, Pedro spotted four dirt bikes coming up the long, steep driveway to the mansion. Following the dirt bikes were two white limousines.

"There he is now," Pedro said. A smile burgeoned on his face. "The man himself."

"That's El Chapo?!" Alana said in disbelief.

Then the unexpected happened.

Something pierced a hole in the window and knocked Pedro to the heated marble floor. Suddenly he could not breathe.

Alana screamed.

Pedro touched a hand to a gaping hole in his chest and felt a warm liquid spilling out.

He looked at the hole in the window and realized he'd been shot. Seconds later he took his last breath.

**

Alexus couldn't remember ever being so happy with her life than she was now.

She and Blake had been together every single day since Mercedes was killed in Chicago that fateful night nine months ago, and not once had she been forced to go ballistic over him cheating with another woman. In fact, Blake had become so faithful that he regularly left his iPhones in her possession without them being locked, something he never did in the past.

She and Blake were sitting in the front row of the 42-seat theater aboard The Omnipotent, the massive megayacht her father had left to her, watching Straight Outta Compton for the first time, when Alexus got the call from Enrique, who'd been staying in Mexico to watch over the Costilla Cartel's operations.

"Cut that phone off, man. This is supposed to be a special night for us," Blake complained, leaning toward Alexus and rubbing a hand on her belly.

She was nine months pregnant. Her due date was technically today, since midnight had just passed.

"It's Enrique," she whispered, as if they were in a public theater full of other movie-goers.

Seated in the rows behind them were Dr. Melonie Farr and her husband, attorney Britney Bostic and her husband, and attorney Nikkia Staples, the woman who was the second partner at the Bostic and Staples law firm.

Alexus answered the call: "Yes, Enrique? Make it quick. I'm on a date, and the movie's just starting."

"It was a good thing that we put those hidden mics in Pedro's mansion. He's been working on a plan to have El Chapo get you taken out in exchange for him sharing our tunnels and submarines."

Alexus gasped for two reasons: the baby kicked in her stomach, and she was stunned by the revelation of Pedro's disloyalty.

"Yeah. Kinda shocked me, too," Enrique said. "I thought he'd be smarter than that after what happened to Mary."

Alexus shook her head. She was doing her best to stay away from the cartel's dealings, but what had to be done could not be avoided.

"Kill him," she whispered.

"It's already done. I did it myself, from two hundred yards away. Same gun I used to hit T-Walk."

"Great."

"You should've seen it. He didn't know what hit him. So, what are you going to do now? Who's going to run things?"

Alexus sighed and looked over at Blake. "You, Enrique. I can't come back. You'll have to be the boss now. Are you okay with that?"

Enrique did not hesitate. "Of course I will. Anything for the queen."

And that is how Enrique became the boss of the most powerful drug cartel in Mexico.

The following morning Alexus gave birth to a healthy nine-pound baby boy. She and Blake named him Juan Costilla King, after her deceased father, and the wealthy couple went on to live a happy life in America while simultaneously masterminding The Costilla Cartel's operations and raising their children together.

A year later, Bulletface became the first rapper to ever go diamond when he released "The White Album", which not surprisingly was all about dealing cocaine.

The End

Lock Down Publications and Ca$h Presents assisted publishing packages.

BASIC PACKAGE $499
Editing
Cover Design
Formatting

UPGRADED PACKAGE $800
Typing
Editing
Cover Design
Formatting

ADVANCE PACKAGE $1,200
Typing
Editing
Cover Design
Formatting
Copyright registration
Proofreading
Upload book to Amazon

LDP SUPREME PACKAGE $1,500
Typing
Editing
Cover Design
Formatting
Copyright registration
Proofreading
Set up Amazon account
Upload book to Amazon
Advertise on LDP Amazon and Facebook page

**Other services available upon request. Additional charges may apply
**Lock Down Publications
P.O. Box 944
Stockbridge, GA 30281-9998
Phone # 470 303-9761**

Submission Guideline

Submit the first three chapters of your completed manuscript to ldpsubmissions@gmail.com, subject line: Your book's title. The manuscript must be in a .doc file and sent as an attachment. Document should be in Times New Roman, double spaced and in size 12 font. Also, provide your synopsis and full contact information. If sending multiple submissions, they must each be in a separate email.

Have a story but no way to send it electronically? You can still submit to LDP/Ca$h Presents. Send in the first three chapters, written or typed, of your completed manuscript to:

LDP: Submissions Dept
Po Box 944
Stockbridge, Ga 30281

DO NOT send original manuscript. Must be a duplicate.

Provide your synopsis and a cover letter containing your full contact information.

Thanks for considering LDP and Ca$h Presents.

NEW RELEASES

THE BLACK DIAMOND CARTEL by SAYNOMORE

THE BIRTH OF A GANGSTER 3 by DELMONT PLAYER

SALUTE MY SAVAGERY by FUMIYA PAYNE

THE COCAINE PRINCESS 10 by KING RIO

BLOOD OF A BOSS **VI**

SHADOWS OF THE GAME II

TRAP BASTARD II

By **Askari**

LOYAL TO THE GAME **IV**

By **T.J. & Jelissa**

TRUE SAVAGE **VIII**

MIDNIGHT CARTEL IV

DOPE BOY MAGIC IV

CITY OF KINGZ III

NIGHTMARE ON SILENT AVE II

THE PLUG OF LIL MEXICO III

CLASSIC CITY II

By **Chris Green**

BLAST FOR ME **III**

A SAVAGE DOPEBOY III

CUTTHROAT MAFIA III

DUFFLE BAG CARTEL VII

HEARTLESS GOON VI

By **Ghost**

A HUSTLER'S DECEIT III

KILL ZONE II

BAE BELONGS TO ME III

TIL DEATH II

By **Aryanna**

KING OF THE TRAP III

By **T.J. Edwards**

GORILLAZ IN THE BAY V

3X KRAZY III

STRAIGHT BEAST MODE III

De'Kari

KINGPIN KILLAZ IV

STREET KINGS III

PAID IN BLOOD III

CARTEL KILLAZ IV

DOPE GODS III

Hood Rich

SINS OF A HUSTLA II

ASAD

YAYO V

Bred In The Game 2

S. Allen

THE STREETS WILL TALK II

By Yolanda Moore

SON OF A DOPE FIEND III

HEAVEN GOT A GHETTO III

SKI MASK MONEY III

By Renta

LOYALTY AIN'T PROMISED III

By Keith Williams

I'M NOTHING WITHOUT HIS LOVE II

SINS OF A THUG II

TO THE THUG I LOVED BEFORE II

IN A HUSTLER I TRUST II

By Monet Dragun

QUIET MONEY IV

EXTENDED CLIP III

Jibril Williams
THUG LIFE IV

By **Trai'Quan**

THE STREETS MADE ME IV

By **Larry D. Wright**

IF YOU CROSS ME ONCE III

ANGEL V

By **Anthony Fields**

THE STREETS WILL NEVER CLOSE IV

By **K'ajji**

HARD AND RUTHLESS III

KILLA KOUNTY IV

By **Khufu**

MONEY GAME III

By **Smoove Dolla**

JACK BOYS VS DOPE BOYS IV

A GANGSTA'S QUR'AN V

COKE GIRLZ II

COKE BOYS II

LIFE OF A SAVAGE V

CHI'RAQ GANGSTAS V

SOSA GANG IV

BRONX SAVAGES II

BODYMORE KINGPINS II

BLOOD OF A GOON II

By **Romell Tukes**

MURDA WAS THE CASE III

Elijah R. Freeman

AN UNFORESEEN LOVE IV

BABY, I'M WINTERTIME COLD III

By **Meesha**

QUEEN OF THE ZOO III

By **Black Migo**

CONFESSIONS OF A JACKBOY III

By Nicholas Lock

KING KILLA II

By Vincent "Vitto" Holloway

BETRAYAL OF A THUG III

By Fre$h

THE BIRTH OF A GANGSTER IV

By Delmont Player

TREAL LOVE II

By Le'Monica Jackson

FOR THE LOVE OF BLOOD IV

By Jamel Mitchell

RAN OFF ON DA PLUG II

By Paper Boi Rari

HOOD CONSIGLIERE III

By Keese

PRETTY GIRLS DO NASTY THINGS II

By Nicole Goosby

LOVE IN THE TRENCHES II

By Corey Robinson

FOREVER GANGSTA III

By Adrian Dulan

SUPER GREMLIN II

By King Rio

CRIME BOSS II

Jibril Williams
Playa Ray

LOYALTY IS EVERYTHING III

Molotti

HERE TODAY GONE TOMORROW II

By Fly Rock

REAL G'S MOVE IN SILENCE II

By Von Diesel

GRIMEY WAYS IV

By Ray Vinci

BLOOD AND GAMES II

By King Dream

THE BLACK DIAMOND CARTEL II

By SayNoMore

<u>Available Now</u>

RESTRAINING ORDER **I & II**

By **CA$H & Coffee**

LOVE KNOWS NO BOUNDARIES **I II & III**

By **Coffee**

RAISED AS A GOON I, II, III & IV

BRED BY THE SLUMS I, II, III

BLAST FOR ME I & II

Jibril Williams
MONEY MAFIA I II

LOYAL TO THE SOIL I II III

By **Jibril Williams**

A DISTINGUISHED THUG STOLE MY HEART I II & III

LOVE SHOULDN'T HURT I II III IV

RENEGADE BOYS I II III IV

PAID IN KARMA I II III

SAVAGE STORMS I II III

AN UNFORESEEN LOVE I II III

BABY, I'M WINTERTIME COLD I II

By **Meesha**

A GANGSTER'S CODE I &, II III

A GANGSTER'S SYN I II III

THE SAVAGE LIFE I II III

CHAINED TO THE STREETS I II III

BLOOD ON THE MONEY I II III

A GANGSTA'S PAIN I II III

By J-Blunt

PUSH IT TO THE LIMIT

By **Bre' Hayes**

BLOOD OF A BOSS **I, II, III, IV, V**

SHADOWS OF THE GAME

TRAP BASTARD

By **Askari**

THE STREETS BLEED MURDER **I, II & III**

THE HEART OF A GANGSTA I II& III

By **Jerry Jackson**

CUM FOR ME I II III IV V VI VII VIII

An **LDP Erotica Collaboration**

216

BRIDE OF A HUSTLA **I II & II**

THE FETTI GIRLS **I, II& III**

CORRUPTED BY A GANGSTA I, II III, IV

BLINDED BY HIS LOVE

THE PRICE YOU PAY FOR LOVE I, II ,III

DOPE GIRL MAGIC I II III

By **Destiny Skai**

WHEN A GOOD GIRL GOES BAD

By **Adrienne**

THE COST OF LOYALTY I II III

By Kweli

A GANGSTER'S REVENGE **I II III & IV**

THE BOSS MAN'S DAUGHTERS I II III IV V

A SAVAGE LOVE **I & II**

BAE BELONGS TO ME I II

A HUSTLER'S DECEIT I, II, III

WHAT BAD BITCHES DO I, II, III

SOUL OF A MONSTER I II III

KILL ZONE

A DOPE BOY'S QUEEN I II III

TIL DEATH

By **Aryanna**

A KINGPIN'S AMBITON

A KINGPIN'S AMBITION **II**

I MURDER FOR THE DOUGH

By **Ambitious**

TRUE SAVAGE I II III IV V VI VII

DOPE BOY MAGIC I, II, III

MIDNIGHT CARTEL I II III

Jibril Williams

Renta

GORILLAZ IN THE BAY **I II III IV**

TEARS OF A GANGSTA I II

3X KRAZY I II

STRAIGHT BEAST MODE I II

DE'KARI

TRIGGADALE I II III

MURDAROBER WAS THE CASE I II

Elijah R. Freeman

GOD BLESS THE TRAPPERS I, II, III

THESE SCANDALOUS STREETS I, II, III

FEAR MY GANGSTA I, II, III IV, V

THESE STREETS DON'T LOVE NOBODY I, II

BURY ME A G I, II, III, IV, V

A GANGSTA'S EMPIRE I, II, III, IV

THE DOPEMAN'S BODYGAURD I II

THE REALEST KILLAZ I II III

THE LAST OF THE OGS I II III

Tranay Adams

THE STREETS ARE CALLING

Duquie Wilson

MARRIED TO A BOSS I II III

By Destiny Skai & Chris Green

KINGZ OF THE GAME I II III IV V VI VII

CRIME BOSS

Playa Ray

SLAUGHTER GANG I II III

RUTHLESS HEART I II III

By Willie Slaughter

FUK SHYT

By Blakk Diamond

DON'T F#CK WITH MY HEART I II

By Linnea

ADDICTED TO THE DRAMA I II III

IN THE ARM OF HIS BOSS II

By Jamila

YAYO I II III IV

A SHOOTER'S AMBITION I II

BRED IN THE GAME

By S. Allen

TRAP GOD I II III

RICH $AVAGE I II III

MONEY IN THE GRAVE I II III

By Martell Troublesome Bolden

FOREVER GANGSTA I II

GLOCKS ON SATIN SHEETS I II

By Adrian Dulan

TOE TAGZ I II III IV

LEVELS TO THIS SHYT I II

IT'S JUST ME AND YOU I II

By Ah'Million

KINGPIN DREAMS I II III

RAN OFF ON DA PLUG

By Paper Boi Rari

CONFESSIONS OF A GANGSTA I II III IV

CONFESSIONS OF A JACKBOY I II

By Nicholas Lock

I'M NOTHING WITHOUT HIS LOVE

QUIET MONEY I II III

THUG LIFE I II III

EXTENDED CLIP I II

A GANGSTA'S PARADISE

By **Trai'Quan**

THE STREETS MADE ME I II III

By **Larry D. Wright**

THE ULTIMATE SACRIFICE I, II, III, IV, V, VI

KHADIFI

IF YOU CROSS ME ONCE I II

ANGEL I II III IV

IN THE BLINK OF AN EYE

By **Anthony Fields**

THE LIFE OF A HOOD STAR

By **Ca$h & Rashia Wilson**

THE STREETS WILL NEVER CLOSE I II III

By **K'ajji**

CREAM I II III

THE STREETS WILL TALK

By **Yolanda Moore**

NIGHTMARES OF A HUSTLA I II III

BLOOD AND GAMES

By **King Dream**

CONCRETE KILLA I II III

VICIOUS LOYALTY I II III

By **Kingpen**

HARD AND RUTHLESS I II

MOB TOWN 251

THE BILLIONAIRE BENTLEYS I II III

GRIMEY WAYS I II III

By Ray Vinci

XMAS WITH AN ATL SHOOTER

By Ca$h & Destiny Skai

KING KILLA

By Vincent "Vitto" Holloway

BETRAYAL OF A THUG I II

By Fre$h

THE MURDER QUEENS I II III

By Michael Gallon

TREAL LOVE

By Le'Monica Jackson

FOR THE LOVE OF BLOOD I II III

By Jamel Mitchell

HOOD CONSIGLIERE I II

By Keese

PROTÉGÉ OF A LEGEND I II III

LOVE IN THE TRENCHES

By Corey Robinson

BORN IN THE GRAVE I II III

By Self Made Tay

MOAN IN MY MOUTH

SANCTIFIED AND HORNY

By XTASY

TORN BETWEEN A GANGSTER AND A GENTLEMAN

By J-BLUNT & Miss Kim

LOYALTY IS EVERYTHING I II

Molotti

HERE TODAY GONE TOMORROW

Jibril Williams
By Fly Rock

PILLOW PRINCESS

By S. Hawkins

NAÏVE TO THE STREETS

WOMEN LIE MEN LIE I II III

GIRLS FALL LIKE DOMINOS

STACK BEFORE YOU SPURLGE

FIFTY SHADES OF SNOW I II III

By A. Roy Milligan

SALUTE MY SAVAGERY I II

By Fumiya Payne

BOOKS BY LDP'S CEO, CA$H

TRUST IN NO MAN

TRUST IN NO MAN 2

TRUST IN NO MAN 3

BONDED BY BLOOD

SHORTY GOT A THUG

THUGS CRY

THUGS CRY 2

THUGS CRY 3

TRUST NO BITCH

TRUST NO BITCH 2

TRUST NO BITCH 3

TIL MY CASKET DROPS

RESTRAINING ORDER

RESTRAINING ORDER 2

IN LOVE WITH A CONVICT

LIFE OF A HOOD STAR

XMAS WITH AN ATL SHOOTER

Jibril Williams

CPSIA information can be obtained
at www.ICGtesting.com
Printed in the USA
LVHW081617090723
751942LV00043B/574